PRAISE FOR LAURENCE SHAMES' NOVELS

"As enjoyable as a day at the beach."

– USA Today

"Funny, suspenseful, romantic, and wise...Shames is a terrific writer with real heart"

—Detroit Free Press

"Expertly blends fast-paced action with colorful dialogue...Smart and consistently entertaining"

—The Chicago Tribune Book Review

"A clever premise is explored with delicious dark humor and healthy cynicism"

—The San Francisco Chronicle

ONE BIG JOKE

LAURENCE SHAMES

Copyright © 2018 Laurence Shames

All rights reserved.

ISBN: 1981614281
ISBN-13: 978-1981614288

DEDICATION

For Marilyn, who keeps me laughing and, I hope, vice-versa

Dying's easy. Comedy is hard.

Edmund Kean, English actor,

on his deathbed in 1833

PART ONE

1

"What is with you lately?" said Marsha Gluck on what might or might not have turned out to be the last evening of her nine-year marriage to the then-unemployed comedy writer Lenny Sullivan. "You've been acting like everything is one big joke."

"That is so not true," he said, but he said it more by reflex than from conviction.

Lenny was forty-two, of average height, average build, with darting hazel eyes and rather kinky and wild brown hair that was just beginning to recede from a tall and often crinkled brow. He had a habit, when conversing, of leaning forward from the waist, then again from the neck. This forward lean helped to quicken his responses and focus his attention. Even so, he didn't really understand exactly how or when this conversation with his wife had begun to curdle into an argument.

"It is true," she insisted. "It is. The worse things get, the grimmer things look, with the politics, the craziness, the country going down the tubes, the more you make it sound like one big joke. To you that's all it is."

"No. Not so. It isn't one big joke. It's a whole lot of little jokes all strung together. Some of them are funnier than others."

"You see? There you go again. Always with the sarcasm, the subversion. I'm getting a little worried about you, Lenny. All this undercutting, this dodging. I'm just not sure it's healthy."

"Dodging what?" he asked, his neck craning forward another inch or two. "What am I dodging?"

"That life is serious. That the world is a serious place."

"And this means it can't also be funny? Marsha, what can I say? I write gags. I make up skits. That's what I do. So call me a lightweight. We can't all be short-listed for a MacArthur. We can't all win the Nobel Prize. We can't all write *The Grapes of* fucking *Wrath*. We can't all be Jean-Paul fucking Sartre. We can't all—"

"Okay, okay, I get the point."

"Do you? All I'm saying, I'm saying that, like practically everybody else, all I'm trying to do is get through another day in your very serious world without a shit-fit or a major depression. So how do I do that? By making jokes. Maybe providing a few laughs for people. Maybe even getting paid for it."

"Except you're not getting paid for it these days."

"Oh, thanks so much for reminding me."

By then he was pacing around the cluttered living room of their small New York apartment. The room's carpet had some wine and coffee stains on it and some of its fringes were unraveling. It looked like crap but they hadn't bothered to replace it because, back when Lenny's career was going better, they'd figured they'd soon be moving to a bigger place, so why accumulate more stuff to shlep around? "Not getting paid," he went on. "Not bringing home the bacon. And I'm sure that's my fault, too."

"Who's talking fault, Lenny? No one's talking fault."

"Yup, definitely my fault that the supposedly ready-to-break-big star of the show I was writing flaked out and went into rehab just before we were supposed to shoot the pilot. Not sure what I did wrong, but it's definitely my fault."

"Can we please stop talking fault? I'm just trying to figure out why you've been in such a bad mood lately. So negative all the time. So gloomy. I mean, you make a lot of jokes but I don't hear you laughing."

This was happening at around ten o'clock on a January night. Marsha was already dressed for bed, wearing fuzzy slippers along with a blue wool bathrobe over mint green pajamas. Lenny, just slightly dizzy from the quick pivots of his pacing, eventually plopped down into an armchair and looked at her while pretending not to. He still loved to look at her, even when he was feeling lousy, even when they were quarreling. She had short cinnamon-colored hair and bright green eyes with yellow flecks. Her hair was so thick that it completely swallowed up the earpieces of her reading glasses; her eyes would twinkle or darken in sympathy or disagreement with whatever she was reading. The book she was holding was, as usual, a thick and heavy one and it made a dent in her lap, and for some reason Lenny found this small and intimate detail heartbreaking.

How many times had he watched her read, seen the different ways she held a book, the way her lips squeezed together when she bent closer to scrawl notes in the margins? Noticing and savoring things like that: Wasn't that a big part of what married love was all about? So just what the hell was happening to the two of them? Why couldn't they seem to get through an evening without an argument? Were they just in a bad patch or were they falling apart, letting their bond be poisoned by some tough and toxic times? When had they stopped laughing together? She used to laugh at his jokes. Often she helped shape them, tune them up. Not lately. Was she losing her regard for what he did? Or maybe he was losing it himself. Was it him? Was it *all* him? Was he just being impossible?

After a minute of dispiriting reflection, he couldn't sit still anymore and he sprang out of his chair. "I've gotta go move the car," he said.

What happened next could, from a certain viewpoint, be blamed on alternate-side-of-the-street parking. Then again, if things had been going better in the comedy business and if Lenny had still been able to afford a garage, alternate-side-of-the-street parking would not have been an issue. Plus Lenny would have been a lot less touchy. So you could also blame what happened next on his being unemployed.

In any case, he went to the bedroom, grabbed his car keys, phone, and wallet, and headed for the door of the apartment.

Without admitting he was doing so, he hesitated there for just a moment, waiting to hear his wife remind him to put a coat on. Lenny often headed out to move the car in winter without first grabbing a coat. This was generally because he was preoccupied, thinking through a skit or polishing a punch line or wondering how to approach a former employer about giving him some work. Usually, just as he was reaching for the doorknob, Marsha would sing out, "Don't forget your coat."

This time she didn't. Maybe it was just a tiny oversight. Maybe she was at a particularly serious spot in her reading. Still, the omission tweaked Lenny's already bruised and maudlin feelings. He thought the worst: Maybe his wife had stopped caring much if he went out without a coat and caught a cold or even pneumonia. Maybe she *wanted* him to catch pneumonia. All right, fuck it then. Bring on the antibiotics, the IV pole, the Filipino nurses. He headed out without a coat.

The hallway of their building depressed him further. It smelled of cabbage and old ladies. The street in front of the building was strewn with dented garbage cans and windblown Chinese take-out menus. For years now, decades, the Upper West Side had been gentrifying. Why did the spiffing up always seem to stop right at their block? Their block was like the dry spot on a lawn that the sprinklers always fell just short of. He found his car. It had been a new car once, a nice car. It wasn't any more. That depressed him too. He unlocked it, got in, and started looking for a new space on the opposite side of the street.

If he'd found one right away, his life would not have changed.

He would have re-parked, gone back upstairs, flossed his teeth, and gotten into bed with a glass of Scotch and a yellow pad. His wife would have joined him at some point. Maybe she would have read in silence until the lights were switched off, or maybe they would have reconciled with a hug and a kiss, maybe even made love or found something to laugh about together.

But he didn't find a parking space.

So he drove around the block. The car was cold, the upholstery chilled his back, and everything annoyed him: the asshole with Jersey plates who'd taken up a space and a half; the fire hydrants that wasted precious swaths of curb; the smug garages filled with the vehicles of people whose luck was running better, who were making even these lousy times work just fine for them.

He went around another block, then another, still planning to lock up and go back to the apartment, but as he spiraled farther out from his building, pinwheeling like a slow and tiny nebula, the gravity that had held his life together seemed somehow to loosen its grip, almost to be casting him off. Traffic light by traffic light it became possible to imagine that maybe he would not go home. Why should he? He'd stopped being sure his wife loved him anymore; he couldn't quite figure why she would. He had fresh and nagging doubts about whether the work he'd been doing for as long as he could remember was of any value whatsoever. Making people laugh. He'd told himself it mattered. But maybe it didn't. Maybe Marsha was right. Maybe the world had gotten awfully serious, terminally serious, and he was out of step. But if his work was trivial and he couldn't make a living from it anyway, and if his wife kept picking on him on top of that, and if they ended up arguing even when neither of them really wanted to, just where the hell did that leave him?

He kept making turns at street corners. Halfheartedly, he kept scanning left and right for an available parking space, but he was no longer looking very hard or seeing very clearly because his eyes had misted over. This was from the cold, he told himself. Only that. From sitting in the cold car without a coat on.

Finally he came to a corner where he didn't make a turn. He was on West End Avenue, heading south, and although he couldn't quite remember making a decision to continue straight ahead, south was where he kept on pointing. After all those blocks and blocks of crawling pinwheels, it felt as free and loose as punch-drunk laughter to be on a straight course, heading somewhere, anywhere.

His spirits giddily if ambivalently rising, the crisis embraced if not fully understood, he pressed down on the accelerator until he was in perfect sync with the traffic lights, and every one of them turned green for him, as though urging him on, wishing him well, clear through to the entrance of the Lincoln Tunnel.

2

In Key West, at a small, uncrowded, and perennially close to bankrupt comedy club called Titters, another week-night open-mic session was slogging along toward its one a.m. conclusion. You never knew what you'd get on open-mic nights, and over the course of the long evening there'd been a handful of good belly laughs, a fair number of cringes, and plenty of those excruciating silences that fill the hopeful then wrist-slitting interval between when a joke leaves a comedian's mouth and when it lands in the ears of an audience that either doesn't get it or just doesn't think it's funny.

The performers and the material had been all over the place. There'd been Trump jokes and dick jokes, parodies of TV shows and shticks about stoned-out Keys types blundering through life. There were a lot of riffs about sex but usually they were about not getting any. There was a routine about socks that got lost in the dryer then mysteriously reappeared on other people's feet in a shadow universe. One woman did a rudely hilarious ten minutes about trying to avoid explaining to her gynecologist how a certain foreign object had ended up lodged where it was.

Between acts, people ordered more drinks. Or at least the proprietor, Pat Coates, hoped they would, because she had rent to pay and licenses to buy and needed every dollar of revenue she could scrape together. Which is why she tended bar herself and also was the one who stacked the chairs and swept the floor when the night was over, and changed the spotlights when they needed changing, and made sure the microphones were fully charged, and did the dozen other little jobs a person never really thought about when hatching the fantasy of owning a small club somewhere.

She'd run Titters for four years now. It never got easier, but she'd promised herself that by the end of her ten-year lease she would have managed, at least, to put the place on the sort of semi-semi-mainstream comedy circuit—make it at least an A-minus or B-plus kind of venue that people would have heard of. The club was in a converted houseboat tied up to a city-owned dock that flanked U.S. 1 at Garrison Bight. There was, of course, a funk and a romance to the whole floating concept, and the dockside tub had always seemed a promising location for *something*, yet every business that leased it had gone belly up. During the ten years Pat had lived in Key West, the place had failed as a Thai restaurant, failed as an art gallery, failed even as a T-shirt shop. Perversely, it was this whiff of failure that had made the spot irresistible to her. A comedy writer and former stand-up herself, she saw comedy and failure as going hand in hand, being natural partners. Jokes, after all, were a way of fighting back from helplessness. Laughing was how people told failure to go fuck itself.

So she kept at it. She felt good about giving young comics a place to hone their craft. She enjoyed—sometimes—schmoozing with the customers, or at least with the small number who were regulars. Like the very old man she was chatting with now.

He was a lean fellow with a good head of silver hair tinged at the ends with the brittle yellow of ancient newspaper. He had a banana nose and fleshy lips and he wore a red silk shirt printed with a bold pattern of classic-shaped cocktail glasses—martini, daiquiri, hi-ball—tipped at various angles. His name was Bert d'Ambrosia, and the rumor—though rumors of scandalous past lives surrounded a lot of people in Key West—was that he was some kind of retired Mafioso. The old man was friendly, sort of relentlessly friendly, and he always had a fidgety chihuahua named Nacho in his lap. He didn't always laugh at the comedy—a lot of the pop culture memes passed him right by—but he never failed to feed the tip jar or to applaud at the end of a set. These people were trying, after all.

"Comedy my day and comedy now," he was saying during the break. "Know the difference?"

Pat was drawing someone a beer. She was tall and angular yet there was also a softness in her looks that came mainly from the mildness of her wide gray eyes. Her hair was short and ash-blond, coarsely cut so that different layers of it overlapped like shingles. It was a way cool haircut, probably a haircut meant for someone younger than her nearly forty years, but she didn't care; she liked it that way. Finally she turned back to Bert and said, "Yeah. Your day, comedy was a bunch of straight white guys in suits and ties standing still as trees and telling corny jokes."

"Corny says you. No. The difference was, my day, everyone agreed on what was funny. Take Jack Benny. Guy never even needed to tell a joke. All he'd do is fold his arms, turn his head a certain way, and say...*Well*...and the entire country was cracked up. Now it's like, I dunno, little territories, ghettos. Ya got jokes for twenty year olds and jokes for sixty year olds, jokes for guys and jokes for women, jokes for straights and jokes for gays, and no one gets it what the other side is laughing at. Plus ya got this whole CP thing—"

"PC."

"Whatever. So you got all this stuff that, deep down, everybody knows is funny but you're not allowed to say it. Like if you don't say it, it'll go away. Which happens to be bullshit. Hypocrisy. S'okay, ya don't wanna hurt no one's feelings. I get it. Fair enough. But come on, ya can't tell an Eyetie joke unless you're an Eyetie? Can't tell a Jew joke unless you're a Jew? Tonto, forget about it. When's the last time you heard a good Lone Ranger joke? All I'm sayin' is—"

Whatever he was saying, it would have to wait, because just then Pat's phone rang. It wasn't the club phone but rather her personal line, and it rang with one of the special tones reserved for close friends who, being in the comedy world, tended to have breakdowns and crises and overdoses in the middle of the night.

This particular tone belonged to her buddy and sometime writing partner Lenny Sullivan. When they were on a project together, they'd call each other at all hours to test out a line, buff up a gag. But they weren't on a project now and so his late-night call was a little bit concerning. She picked up, and through the hum of the club, said, "Lenny?"

He said, "It's Lenny."

"I know. I just said that."

"I'm in Delaware."

"Delaware? Fascinating. Have you done an Instagram post?"

"I think I just walked out on Marsha."

"You *what?*"

"I didn't mean to. I was in a crappy mood. I went to move the car. Then I was on the Turnpike. I don't know exactly how it happened."

Pat said nothing.

"She's been pretty tough on me lately," Lenny rambled. "Or at least that's how it feels. Probably I deserve it. Probably when I don't have work I'm a pain to be around. Hold on, I'm coming to a toll."

Pat moved the phone to arm's length and looked up at the stage. A comedian was talking about her secret desire to sneak up behind old guys who drive Harleys and snip off their silver ponytails. The notion got a few sparse laughs.

Lenny came back on the line and said, "I think I just crossed over into Maryland."

"Wow, that's really something. Have you considered a gig on the Travel Channel?"

He said, "Pat, I'm a mess. I really don't know what to do right now."

"I think you do," his old friend said. "I think you know exactly what to do and in fact I think you're doing it. You should drive to Key West, spend some time with Sam and me, and figure it out from there."

"Jeez. Really? Well, I didn't mean to...You really think that would be okay?"

"No, I think it'll suck. But what can I say? You're in Maryland. Practically just around the corner. A measly thousand miles, give or take. Of course come stay with us awhile."

Gratitude choked him up and for some seconds he just drove down the mostly empty highway in silence. Then, a propos of nothing, just wanting to stay on the line with a friend, he said, "That pilot we wrote a few months ago. It was damn good. Like, six seasons good."

"Had possibilities," she said mildly. She didn't want to get worked up about it, put herself through the frustration and disappointment all over again.

"*Dog Groomer to the Stars,*" Lenny murmured wistfully. Then, leaning forward in that way he had, even when on the phone in his car somewhere in Maryland, he went on. "Had possibilities? Shit, it had everything! The salon setting. Mega-diversity in the ensemble of groomers. Cute dogs. Endless opportunities for cameo appearances. And the head groomer, Alonzo—what an opportunity for a rising comedian, a fresh face. If only that charming asshole Ricky hadn't picked that moment to go running into rehab."

Pat didn't respond to that. She was trying to give at least part of her attention and sympathy to a comic who was bombing badly with a hip-hop version of a Cialis ad.

"The weird part?" Lenny rambled on from the lonely darkness of the highway. "His leaving, the rehab thing, it was so abrupt. Like out of nowhere. He didn't even seem that strung out to me. I mean, not compared to a lot of other guys at least. Did he to you?"

Pat didn't reply to that either. She didn't reply because just then the door to her little club swung violently open and a naked man came storming in.

The naked guy was kind of short but reasonably buff, and tan from head to toe, though the tan had an unnatural coppery-vermilion sheen to it, especially on his well-toned buttocks. He was wearing a cheap and spiky plastic wig and large round sunglasses with thick white frames.

Taking long, low steps like Groucho Marx, he bounded up onto the stage, seized the mic from the flabbergasted comic who'd been failing with the hip-hop thing, and sang the first few words of *The Star-Spangled Banner* to the tune of *Happy Birthday*. Then he sang the first few words of *Happy Birthday* to the tune of *The Star-Spangled Banner*. Then he quietly handed the microphone back, jumped down off the stage and ran out the way he'd entered.

There was a moment of stunned silence as the door slammed shut behind his tinted posterior. Then, uneasily at first, then more wholeheartedly, people started to laugh. They were in a comedy club, after all, and they were in Key West, and it was nearly one a.m. They thought the crazy naked guy was one more part of the show.

At the bar, the old man named Bert shook his head, petted his dog, and said, "Christ, never seen an act quite like that before. Gimme Bob Hope any day."

Into the phone, Pat said to Lenny, "Look, I gotta go. Something very strange just happened."

"Strange, like, how?"

"Strange, like, bizarre. Like, a naked guy running in off the street and doing a routine that lasted twenty seconds."

That cheered Lenny up a little. In such a serious world, how could you not treasure stuff like that? "Open-mic night," he said. "Gotta love it."

"Well...yeah," said Pat. She hesitated, seemed to be deciding against saying something then said it anyway. "But I got kind of an odd question for you. Our pal Ricky. Ever see him naked?"

"Ricky? Naked? Of course I haven't seen him naked. Why?"

"Well, the guy who just streaked my club reminded me an awful lot of him. Manic like Ricky. Same size and build, except he had an orange ass."

"Lots of guys are manic and I have no idea what color Ricky's ass is, but I know he can't be naked at your club because he's in rehab in a fancy detox joint just outside of Princeton."

"I know he is," said Pat. "Or at least I think I know. And I'm sure you're right. Must've been just some other random naked guy...And I guess it's just a coincidence that he did a riff from one of our old skits."

"One of our skits?"

"Look, I gotta go. Gotta do last call and then I could really use a drink myself. Drive safe. See ya when I see ya."

3

A day and a half later, an unshaven and red-eyed Lenny pulled up in front of Pat and Sam's little yellow house on Pine Street.

He'd visited a couple times before and always loved it. Loved everything about it, really: The shady porch with the funky wicker furniture that little curls of wicker were always breaking off of; the way sunlight came in golden horizontal stripes through the shutters on the living room windows; the narrow side yard so choked with crotons and low sedges that it made even the shortest stroll seem like a trek through the jungle. Every time he'd visited Key West, he'd gone home asking himself why he didn't get the hell out of New York and move down to a little house like that. Though he never quite succeeded in answering the question, he sort of suspected it was because living in a little house like that might make him more relaxed and maybe even happy, and contentment might dull the edge of his subversive tendencies, and apparently that scared him.

Now he walked up the three cheerily creaking steps that led to the front door. Only the screen was closed and he could see clear through the living room and kitchen to the compact backyard with its buttonwood hedge and small turquoise patch of swimming pool. That was another thing he loved about Pat's house—that you could look right through it, it didn't blot out the day the way big houses or apartment buildings did; it was more like just a brief parenthesis in a long flowing sentence with spacious outdoor clauses both before and after it.

He pressed his nose against the screen and sang out a hello. Pat came through the French doors at the back of the house and gestured him in. They fell into a hug then stood back for a good look at one another. "You look fabulous," he told her. "Tan and fit in January. Life is so not fair."

"And you look like hell," she said. "Want some lunch? Shrimp and avocado."

He didn't know he was going to sigh at that, but he did, deeply. Shrimp and avocado. Out in the sunshine. In the dead of winter. As opposed to the thin soup and skinny sandwich he might have been eating in the Greek joint on Broadway with everybody sweating in the steam heat beneath their heavy clothes. Just why was he living his life the way he'd been living it? Why was he making it more unpleasant than it had to be?

A few minutes later, sitting at a small table next to the pool, a plate of chilled pink seafood glistening in front of him, he asked how Sam was.

"Sam's great. Busy. On the court six, seven hours a day. Lots of lessons this time of year."

Between bites of crisp shrimp and satiny avocado, he said, "Ya know, sometimes it still surprises me a little."

Pat had had her own lunch a while before. She watched him eat. "What? You think I'm the first person who ever went on vacation and fell in love with her tennis pro?"

He shrugged. "I didn't know you liked the game that much."

"I didn't. Then I did."

"And I guess I never really thought you'd end up with a woman."

"Surprise!"

"You happy?"

"Very."

"I'm glad. I really am. But hey, remember when we used to flirt? Before Marsha? Before Sam?"

"Of course I remember. It was fun. Sort of."

"We even necked a little bit."

"Yeah, I remember that too."

"Is that what made you go gay? Necking with me?"

"You're such an asshole."

"No, I just mean, ya know, you didn't exactly find it thrilling."

"Thrilling? Not in the least. You?"

He chased a slippery piece of avocado around his plate with a fork. "Well, that's the funny part. I didn't either. I felt like I should have. I thought you were beautiful and all. But did I find it thrilling? No. Sorry."

"I'm not. Want some mango for dessert?"

"Mango," he intoned, as though the word were part of some sacred chant. "Pat, you're killin' me here. Mango. Avocado. What's the temperature, like eighty-two degrees? Mind if I take my shirt off?"

"Make yourself at home," she said, and went into the kitchen to cut up some fruit.

By the time she returned he'd shifted his chair to get some sun directly on his shoulders.

"Christ, you're pale," she said. "And if you don't mind my saying so, I'd say maybe it's time to renew your gym membership. Get a little tone back."

"Oh, thank you. Thanks a lot." He stabbed at a chunk of mango. It slid off his fork, as mango will.

She picked hers up with her fingers. "So I have to ask. Have you spoken to Marsha?"

"Sure. I called last night from the road."

"She upset?"

"Yeah, I guess she's upset." He said nothing more. Saying nothing more was very unusual for Lenny.

"Hey, if you don't want to talk about it..."

That made it irresistible to go on. "I just wish I knew what the hell to say. We've been arguing a lot. Not the usual friendly sparring. There's been an edge to it. And at some point I guess I got the feeling..." He paused as though a bit of mango had stuck in his throat even though he knew that the mango had slid right down. "I guess I got this deathly feeling that maybe she just doesn't love me anymore."

Pat reached over and touched the back of his hand. "I doubt that, Lenny. I've known the two of you a long time."

"She doesn't laugh at my jokes."

"Maybe they're not funny."

"Is that supposed to make me feel better?"

"Or maybe she's just not in the mood to laugh. A lot of people aren't these days. It's one more wedge. Black and white, rich and poor, young and old. Now we've also got the laughers and the non-laughers."

"Fine. But she's my wife and making people laugh is what I do."

"Right, and she's a professor, and taking things very seriously is what *they* do. It's just a different approach to feeling helpless. You know what I think, Lenny? I think giving yourself a little time away is the right thing to do. Get some perspective back. Remember how well you two balance each other. Yin and yang."

"Which of those is the funny one? I can't ever remember."

She let that pass and came up with an abrupt segue instead. "But in the meantime, I think we need to talk about this business of Ricky possibly showing up naked at my club."

Lenny leaned forward to meet the change of subject and crisply volleyed it back. "Which didn't happen. Which couldn't have happened.

It couldn't have been Ricky."

"Okay, it couldn't have been Ricky. But there's this small coincidence that needs explaining. Do you remember the day, oh, maybe a year or so ago, I was up in New York, we were working over at your place, and stuff just wasn't coming, wasn't building, wasn't funny."

"That could've been a lot of days."

"Yeah, but this day was especially bad. Really frustrating. So we just started pissing around, trying anything. At some point you sprang out of your chair and started singing *The Star-Spangled Banner* and I started singing *Happy Birthday*, and we realized that the lyrics were exactly interchangeable."

"Right!" Lenny recalled, perking up at the memory. "Six syllables a line, pretty much all the way through. *Oh-oh say can you see...Happy birthday to you.* It was scary how well they fit together."

"Exactly. So you sang the anthem to the tune of the birthday song, and I sang the birthday song to the tune of the anthem, and the funny part was that after a while we both lost track of which song was which. The swapped versions just got stuck in our heads. So we started messing around with how to turn that into a routine, remember?"

"Course I do. Like what if they did the *Happy Birthday* version at football games? Would anyone give a shit if they took a knee? Or what if four-year olds at a party had to sing the anthem before somebody cut the cake? Could've been some funny stuff."

"Could've been," said Pat. "But remember what happened to the idea?"

"Do I remember?" Lenny echoed, with more than a trace of bitterness. "Sure I remember. The studio shot it down. Thought it might be seen as unpatriotic. I couldn't believe it. I mean, please, folks, lighten up. I tried like hell to sell it. Got us nowhere."

Pat pushed aside the last of her mango and leaned across the little table. "Do you remember who was at the meeting when that happened, Lenny?"

"Yeah. Us. A couple other writers. The suits—"

"And Ricky. The suits had called him in because he'd been dissing some of the sponsors, remember? He was next on the agenda."

"So?"

"So Ricky knew about the song routine. Which never aired. That no one ever heard. That never got beyond that conference room. Cut to last night at the club. A naked guy about the size and build of Ricky, except with a crazy wig and giant shades, comes barging in and does basically that same routine. Coincidence? I mean, really, what are the odds?"

Lenny said, "You really think no one else ever noticed how well those two songs go together?"

"I have no idea what other people notice. Lots of people notice that South America sort of fits in to Africa. So what? My question is, have you ever actually heard anybody else sing the *Star-Spangled Banner* to the tune of *Happy Birthday* and vice-versa?"

Lenny had to admit that he hadn't, and that gave him pause. But he still resisted the slim possibility that Ricky Reed was in Key West. He didn't *want* Ricky to be in Key West. He had enough troubles of his own, and he thought he should be entitled to suffer through them in peace. He'd fled to Florida because his life was falling apart. Couldn't he at least have the satisfaction of starring in his own collapse? Couldn't he savor his personal crisis without competition from a high-wattage and high-maintenance near-celebrity whose shenanigans would probably upstage him? Softly but stubbornly, hopefully, he said, "Pat, Ricky's in rehab in New Jersey."

"Okay. Right. And how do we know that? Who'd we hear it from?"

"From everybody. His agent. His manager. His publicist."

"Exactly. Three polished and well-paid liars who decide what the story should be and then stick to it."

"But it was in *Variety*. It was in *The Hollywood Reporter*."

"Who get their inside info where? I rest my case. Look, maybe he's really in rehab. Maybe this was just a naked lookalike. But you know and I know that this whole rehab story could equally well be some kind of ruse, some kind of smokescreen."

"Smokescreen for what?"

She shrugged. The shrug showed off the pretty arc of her collarbones and the bounciness of her layered haircut. "Who knows? But in the meantime I have a theory. What happens when a stranger suddenly appears naked in public?"

"People look," said Lenny.

"Do they? That's what I'm not so sure about. I mean, yeah, people take that first shocked gawk. By reflex. But I think then they get embarrassed and look away. So the nakedness has time to register but the rest of the person really doesn't. The person's kind of invisible."

"So going naked is a kind of low-budget disguise?"

"In a way, yeah, absolutely. Who looks at the face? Then you add in the fake tan, the weird hair-do, the geeky glasses. It's a pretty good incognito."

"Wait, hold on a minute. So now you're saying Ricky Reed stormed into your club stark naked because he didn't want to be recognized?"

"I'm saying it's a possibility."

"But if you don't want to be recognized, isn't it easier just to stay at home with your clothes on? Why would he come in at all?"

At that she crossed her arms and tilted her head into a posture of slightly exasperated patience. "Isn't it obvious?"

"Obvious? No. Call me slow. Road-weary. Preoccupied with my own piddling problems such as going broke and leaving my wife and losing any sense of meaning or purpose in my life. So excuse me, to me none of this is obvious."

"He wanted to be recognized by *me*," said Pat. "Me and no one else. Why else would he have done the anthem routine? He knew I'd be the only one to get it. It was a signal, a cry for help."

The back of Lenny's neck was already getting sunburned and he shifted his chair a few inches before answering. "No. Nuh-uh. I'm sorry, I just don't see where singing *The Star-Spangled Banner* naked is a cry for help."

Softly but firmly, she said, "He's in trouble, Lenny. I feel it. He didn't dash up onto that stage for a couple of quick, cheap laughs. He did it to reach out. To make contact. He's afraid of something. Very afraid. You could feel it all through the room."

Lenny considered that. He rubbed his unshaven jaw and savored the feel of the moist and mild tropical air against his newly liberated skin. A light breeze was rattling the palms. White birds and yellow butterflies flew past. The world in that moment seemed pretty well devoid of menace. Finally he said, "Aren't we getting a little over-dramatic here? I mean, Ricky's a little high-strung, sure, a little flighty, but basically a nice kid with a pretty damn good future ahead of him. What the hell's he got to be afraid of?"

4

In New York, at the Gatto Nero Social Club on Thompson Street in Greenwich Village, Carmine da Silva was tapping an eight-ball against the thin scuffed felt of the pool table where no one had actually shot pool in years. The cue sticks had warped, their tips knocked off-center by break-shots that were hit too hard but without precision; dried-out cubes of blue chalk, now crumbly in their paper wrappers, littered the table's rails.

The Club itself was located behind iron grates a couple of steps below sidewalk level, and as the old brownstone it was housed in had settled more deeply into the bedrock of Manhattan, its floor had tilted in a complex way that seemed to involve several different planes. So the balls no longer rolled straight and this was very frustrating; it made the game seem more like one of sheer dumb luck than skill, and sometimes, when guys had had a few drinks or maybe were a little hopped up on something, and the luck seemed to be all against them in a way that was patently unfair and even cruel, they sometimes got angry and came pretty close to fighting. So it had been decided there'd be no more pool games, at least until the table was leveled, but somehow that had never gotten done.

For a long time, then, the pool table had basically been furniture. Guys leaned against it when they were sipping their espresso and occasionally rested their guns and knives on it when they unburdened themselves of shoulder holsters and ankle sheaths. But a few balls were still arrayed around the felt, and toying with them, rolling them around, feeling their cool slickness against your palm, remained a pretty decent way of shedding extra tension.

Which is what Carmine da Silva was doing now. The eight-ball looked very black and tiny in his huge pink hand as he kept tapping it rhythmically against the felt. He was saying, "My mind, on'y real question left is do I just whack him or do I whack the both of 'em?"

"Her too?" said his friend Peppers Carlucci. Peppers was called Peppers because he ate them at every meal. Sometimes sweet, sometimes hot, but constantly. Breakfast, in with the eggs. Lunch, piled on the sandwich. Dinner, on top of the pasta or seafood or whatever. He asked for them special at every restaurant. Sometimes he carried his own in a small jar in an inner pocket. "Nah, I don't think you could do that, Carmine. Whack a woman, I mean. I couldn't either. There's limits, after all."

"Yeah, you're right, there's limits," the brooding man admitted grudgingly. "Sometimes I wish there wasn't, but there is."

"Besides, you used to be pretty crazy about her."

"Used to be is right. Fuck did it get me? I treated her good. Better'n she deserved, ya want the truth. Clothes, champagne. Nice apartment. True, it was a walk-up, but come on, she got legs. If I can climb the fucking stairs, so can she. Christ, what? All of a sudden she's too good to climb the fucking stairs?"

Peppers said nothing. He didn't think it was about the stairs.

Almost wistfully, Carmine said, "I dunno. Maybe I shoulda gone the extra couple hundred bucks a month and put 'er in an elevator building. Ya think she woulda been happier with an elevator?"

Peppers just shrugged. He didn't think an elevator or an escalator or a helicopter or a rocket ship would have changed the fact that Carmine's squeeze got sick and tired of their whole arrangement and went off with someone else.

"The part that frosts me?" Carmine went on. "What really frosts me is I ask her why. Why this guy? Why *him*? And ya know what she says to me? Because he makes me laugh. Well, that really made *me* laugh. He makes you *laugh*? This is what a man, a lover, is supposed to do? Make you laugh? How about taking care of you, protecting you, buying you stuff, keeping you happy between the legs. That don't count no more?"

Peppers, trying to help, said, "Maybe he'll run outa jokes. Second, third time through, maybe they won't seem so funny."

Carmine tapped the eight-ball harder against the table. "And it's not like I'm an unforgiving guy. Hey, we all make mistakes. I was big about it, I offered her another chance. Drop this clown, I tell her. You like to laugh so much, I'll get ya a pet monkey. *That* she doesn't find funny. Some fuckin' sense a humor, right?"

Peppers said, "Maybe it's just a whaddyacallit, an infatuation with the show business thing. I mean, let's face it, Carmine, maybe that struck her as kinda glamorous."

"Glamorous," echoed Carmine with a derisive snort, now squeezing the pool ball as though trying to compress it into a diamond. "Glamorous my ass. Come on, it's not like the guy's a freakin' movie star. He's been on a coupla TV shows. Stupid ones. Not even network. Cable. Cable shit inna middle of the night. Where's the fuckin' glamour in that?"

"I'm just sayin'—"

"Plus which, now it turns out he's an addict just like the resta those pill-popping misfit geeks. Off to rehab with the other bedwetting losers. Rated exactly two lines on Page Six. *Up and coming comic Ricky Reed goes off to detox.* Guess that tells you what a big star he is. Two stinkin' lines. Runner-ups at the dog show get more'n that."

Peppers thought it was actually pretty cool to get any kind of mention in the paper anywhere except the crime columns, but he kept that to himself.

"Well, I'll tell ya somethin'," Carmine went on, seeming to chew his cheek as he spat out the words, "he went off to rehab just in time. He's damn lucky to be sitting in a nightgown in some rubber room with guards around it, otherwise he'd be dead by now. Just wait'll he gets out. Wait'll I find him. I'll rip his balls off. I'll make him want his pain pills back big time. Funny man. See how funny he is with his nut-sack shredded like linguine."

Peppers, a peaceable man at heart if not always under the pressure of circumstance, secretly winced at the image. Then he said, "Well, who knows, Carmine? Maybe by the time he's back on the street, you'll calm down, it won't seem like a big deal. Maybe you'll be over it altogether. Chances are you'll have a new girlfriend by then."

"I don't want a new girlfriend." He didn't mean to say this; it just came out and he wished it hadn't. He hoped it didn't sound whiny or mopey. Carmine was six-two and a close-packed two hundred thirty pounds. He had a big chin, a broad nose, and the puffy, well-insulated eye sockets of a fighting dog. He'd been bred for toughness; other guys respected him for that, but the downside was that he was expected to maintain his public mojo at all times. Showing even a moment's weakness was an embarrassment not only to himself but to all the guys who looked to him as a model of unwavering and unfeeling strength.

Still, the undeniable truth was that he was still in love with Carla Faletti and he knew deep down that it would not be easy to replace her. Exactly why this was, was a mystery. What made her so special? She was beautiful, sure, with raven hair and bright onyx eyes below steeply arched brows; but lots of women were beautiful. She was electric in the sack—taut in the torso, clinching with the legs—but those things were sort of standard issue in a mistress. Nice boobs, check; good fingernails, tasty lipstick, check and check.

But there was something else that Carla had, something unexpected, outside the usual profile, that had made him happy in her company, at moments even thoroughly content, that had given him a blessed respite from the stress of trying so hard to be who he was. And now, too late, he thought he understood what that special something was, and it turned out to be the most galling thing imaginable.

It was her laugh.

Carla's laugh wasn't loud but it was wholehearted, sudden, irresistible. It started deep in her throat and then sprang forth with a faint little pop of her lips. It was more than a chuckle, less than a roar, the sound of it was deeper than a tinkle, lighter than a guffaw. The laugh was hers alone, and contagious, and her new boyfriend apparently made it happen a lot more often than Carmine ever had, and that's what Carmine couldn't stand. It was a jealousy beyond sex, beyond money, beyond power, beyond anything that Carmine could compete with, and the only possible cure for it was to stop this guy from being so damn amusing by killing him.

"You say that now," answered Peppers.

"Hm?" said Carmine. To him, wrapped up in his morose and violent thoughts, the words seemed to come from some distance away and they took a moment to penetrate.

"That you don't want another girlfriend. You say that now. You'll change your mind. You'll see some babe in a restaurant, a club, she'll look at you a certain way, you'll feel that little twinge in Mr. Friendly, you'll send over a bottle of champagne..."

Carmine tried to smile at that. He dimly realized that his friend was offering him a way to backpedal, to erase his brief display of sentiment, of hurt.

"And inna meantime," Peppers continued, "life goes on. Like always. What, it's gonna stop just 'cause you feel bad about some piece of ass? So be philosophical—don't think about it. Don't get all distracted. That's the main thing. There's stuff to do. Money. Opportunities. Like this Cuba thing."

"Cuba thing? What Cuba thing?"

"Oh Christ, you really are distracted. What Cuba thing? The Cuba thing I mentioned to you yesterday. The thing Fat Lou wants to meet with us about. You really don't remember?"

"Oh yeah," lied Carmine. "Now I do. Sure I do." He nodded unconvincingly, then turned his hand upward and let the eight-ball roll across his palm and down the chute of his fingers. It clicked onto the felt and wobbled slightly as it rolled close to the rail toward a corner pocket. At the last moment it veered just slightly to the left, bumped against a warp in the cushion, and didn't go in.

5

Lenny had lain down for a ten-minute nap in the poolside guest cottage that was little more than a glorified cabana with a tiny bathroom added on, and two hours later he woke up to the smell of frangipani carried on a soft breeze that was the same temperature as his skin, and a baffling but serene sense of dislocation and freedom that made him doubt the old adage that you couldn't run away from your problems.

Who said you couldn't? And why not?

Maybe your problems wouldn't exactly get solved by running away, but maybe they weren't meant to be solved. And what did *solved* mean anyway? Crossword puzzles got solved. Murder mysteries in books got solved. But ordinary problems in ordinary lives played out in ways that were far more complicated and less clear-cut than just solved or unsolved. Ordinary problems in, say, a marriage or a career or life in a city where living was hard, were seldom *solved*, they were dealt with. Or not. Resigned to. Or not. Acknowledged as things to be worked on or ignored as long as possible and then just kicked down the road until the road gave out.

The catch, of course, was that as soon as you turned your back on one set of problems, another set was likely to be staring you in the face. And brand new problems, just because they were new, tended to seem not necessarily more important but certainly more urgent. Was Lenny's old life over? That was a big question, but it could wait. In the meantime, there was the gnawing riddle of what, if anything, was up with Ricky Reed.

Lenny washed his face and went over to the main house, where he found Pat sitting in the small but sunny room she used as her office. She was paying bills, peering through little half-round glasses as she wrote out checks. He couldn't remember ever seeing her with reading glasses before. The peepers reminded him that they'd been friends a helluva long time and weren't exactly kids anymore. He paused in the doorway of the room and without any lead-in whatsoever, he said, "So you really think it was Ricky? You still think that?"

She slid the glasses off her nose and let them dangle from the light chain around her neck. "What I think is that it's the only explanation that even comes close to making sense."

Lenny leaned into his reply. "Okay, but we're dealing with comedians and we're in Key West. Maybe making sense does not apply."

"Usual, everyday, normal sense does not apply. But we're not talking normal here."

He considered that, then surprised himself by saying, "S'okay, say it was Ricky. What the hell are we supposed to do about it?"

Until the words had left his mouth, it hadn't occurred to him that he was supposed to do anything at all. By nature he was an observer, a commentator, a kibitzer, not a man of action. Besides, why would he stick his neck out to help Ricky Reed, if it even *was* Ricky Reed, and if he even needed help? Who, really, was Ricky Reed to him, other than the guy who'd brought him to his nearest near-miss as the co-lead writer of an actual TV series, and who then had dashed his hopes and spoiled everything by flaking out? If anything, Lenny should feel like poking Ricky Reed in the eye with a sharp stick.

Except he didn't feel that way, and he wasn't quite sure why. Maybe it was just that Pat's reading glasses made him feel suddenly oldish, made him acknowledge that maybe it was getting to be his turn to be the grownup. In any case, he found himself feeling oddly if grudgingly protective of Ricky and dimly wondering if he'd end up with some role to play in the younger man's troubles. Big brother? No, way too much responsibility. Mentor? Lacking qualifications. Nice-guy colleague with some life-experience to pass along? That much, maybe he could do.

For some instants, this unexpected impulse to help was simple and pure. But even the purest human motives have a way of becoming quickly tainted by self-interest, and over the course of a couple of heartbeats it dawned on Lenny that helping to fix whatever kind of mess Ricky had got himself into could be a very good thing for himself as well. If Ricky was only in some near-term trouble rather than off to a long stint of rehab, then maybe, just maybe, there'd still be time to shoot the pilot of their show. It was a huge long shot, maybe just a fantasy. But what the hell, why not fantasize? If the pilot got made and the show got green-lighted and caught on, Lenny would be in the chips and in demand. How sweet would that be? A hit would pay for the bigger apartment that he and Marsha had been promising themselves for years. That's right, him and Marsha. Some success would probably help patch things up. His gloom would lift, his confidence rebound, his wife would see the worth of what he did and they'd start laughing together once again...

Lost in his daydream, he only half-heard when Pat said, "Do? I don't think we can do anything for now."

"Hmm?"

"About Ricky. I mean, if it was him, I have to believe he'll be back. If he doesn't come back, then I guess it wasn't him."

"Makes sense," Lenny conceded.

"Even with comedians and even in Key West," said Pat, parking the reading glasses on her nose again. She looked at her old pal over the tops of them. He was carrying his shoulders way too high, almost at the level of his earlobes. The skin looked tight around the hazel eyes but a little flaccid at the jawline. She said, "I really think you could use a little exercise. Want to borrow some tennis gear?"

6

The meeting to which Carmine and Peppers had been summoned was held in the back room of a restaurant just south of Houston Street. This private lair was separated from the public dining area by nothing more than a curtain with a loud pattern of pink roses, so Luigi Benedetti—aka the Old Bastard, aka Raccoon, but mostly aka Fat Lou—had thought it prudent to station a pair of guards on the flanks of the narrow doorway.

On the face of it, though, there really wasn't much to protect in the private dining room. Eight ill-assorted and mostly unhealthy-looking guys sat around a slightly rickety table with a red checkered tablecloth stretched over it. Bottles of Chianti and baskets of bread were arrayed in easy reach. In front of each man was a huge plate of *scungilli* drowned in red sauce over a bed of peppery *biscotti*. The sauce was plenty spicy, but Peppers asked for extra peppers anyway. The yellow ones made a nice contrast with the bright red gravy.

Fat Lou—boss of the Tortelli crime family, or what was left of it after multiple FBI busts, rat-outs, defections, and untimely deaths—sat at the head of the table, his chair placed well back to accommodate his enormous stomach. He had a vast napkin tucked beneath his chin and it swelled across his belly like a spinnaker. He swallowed an epic mouthful of food and washed it down with a lip-smacking gulp of wine.

Then he said to his underlings, "So you twats think you've lived big? You been to Vegas, you been to Miami, you think you've seen it all?

Well, lemme tell ya somethin'. Wit'out you saw Havana before that asshole Castro took it over, you ain't seen shit. For us, for our friends, Havana was home away from home. 'Cept better. No cops. No wives. No competition. Casinos, liquor, construction, we made money on everything. And the broads! Christ, the showgirls, the hookers, hottest in the world. Even the little number who lit your cigar for ya looked like Lana Turner."

He broke off for another Homeric bite of food. While he was chewing, working the hunk of *scungilli* around to the side of his mouth where his teeth were better, Carmine and Peppers shared what they thought was a secret glance. They'd been to meetings like this before and they were a little tired of being lectured about how great things were back when Fat Lou was a young man and they themselves had not been born yet and therefore had missed out.

But the old boss had not survived and stayed on top till the age of eighty-six without being pretty damn savvy. Even through his somewhat milky eyes with the dark bags shaped like Chinese dumplings underneath them, he managed to see everything. Including the impatient and slightly condescending glances of his crew. After a swig of wine he went on, "I know what you cheesedicks are thinkin'. Ya think I don't? You're thinkin' this is just nostalgia, like I imagine Havana is somehow gonna go back to bein' like it was. Well, it isn't. I know that. Nothin' ever goes back like it was."

Here he paused for effect. He lifted his napkin, dabbed his lips, let it flutter down again like a shaken quilt onto a king-size bed.

"No. I have a different reason for tellin' stories about Havana. Not because it's gonna be like it was. Because it's gonna be *better* than it was. Why? Numbers. Old days, a few DC-3s and a coupla cruises a week made it to Cuba. Now ya got 747s and gigantic ships arriving every day. More suckers, more money. Do the math. But that's not the best part. The best part is that we're gonna have our own special way of bringin' suckers in. We're gonna run a ferry service from Key West."

The announcement was met with polite nods but a nearly complete lack of enthusiasm. Fat Lou didn't seem to mind. He went back to his cooling plate of food. The red sauce had soaked into the *biscotti,* giving them a spongy, squishy texture. He squeezed the juice out of them out with his tongue against the roof of his mouth then burped demurely into his fist.

"I can see from your blank expressions," he went on, "that you tits don't have enough imagination to see the full beauty of this idea. You think we're gettin' into the boat-ride business. Well, we'll make some money on the boat ride, sure. And on the marks we bring to the casinos too. But that's the least of it. Think about it, fellas. It's mainly a huge smuggling operation. In both directions. In broad daylight. With a big beautiful boat full of suckers paying gas money. All we do, we pay off a few guys at either end, and we operate open as FedEx. What do we smuggle in? Anything! These people got nothin'. There's black markets for everything. Meat, batteries, Kotex, you name it. Smuggling out? You're thinkin' cigars and rum, right? Nah, that's old hat, nickel-dime. I'm talkin' art, refugees, baseball players. You have any idea how much one stinkin' shortstop goes for? We'll make a freakin' fortune."

At that, unconsciously, the men around the table all picked up their napkins and wiped their watering mouths.

The boss gripped the edge of the table with his fat hands and continued. "There's just one problem and it's screwin' everything up. We don't have space for a terminal in Key West. The cruise lines, the Coast Guard, they got the rights to mosta the docks all sewn up. There's a city dock that's leased out for five, six more years. Ya know what's gonna happen over the course of five, six years? Some legit operation's gonna open up, and that's the end of our opportunity. So we need that dock space sooner. A lot sooner. We got a local partner. Very successful guy, very powerful. Name's Clifton. Ted Clifton. Owns the little tourist train they got down there. Southernmost Choo-Choo. Owns a buncha other things too. Well-connected. He thinks he can make it happen. But he needs help. Like, persuading kind of help. Could get messy. Could get nasty."

He paused, burped, and panned his baggy-eyed gaze around the table. "S'okay, who wants to go?"

7

Armed with Pat's oversized racquet and wearing a pair of shorts close enough to unisex to pass muster in Key West, Lenny walked the three shady blocks to Bayview Park, where Samantha Evans, though no one ever called her that, had been the pro for many years.

It was a City gig, and a pretty good one. Sam gave lessons, strung racquets and sold balls from her very compact pro shop that was basically a shed. In exchange for the concession, it was her responsibility to keep the peace on the five-court complex and to enforce the usual codes of behavior including bans on smoking, drinking, screaming, heckling, using foul language, wearing inappropriate attire, and playing more than one set when others were waiting.

These were basic commonsense rules but the notion of enforcing them in Key West was, of course, a joke. People smoked cigarettes and reefer in the bleachers and brought beers out onto the court in koozies. Large tourist women played in bikinis, breasts jiggling like underdone poached eggs. Local kibitzers set up lawn chairs just outside the fence and loudly predicted double-faults at key junctures. Strategies for court-hogging were almost an art.

Mostly, Sam just shrugged off the daily violations. This wasn't Wimbledon, after all. People played shirtless, dropped f-bombs when they missed a shot, now and then chucked racquets. So what? On the rare occasions when things threatened to get really out of hand, Sam would walk over and restore order without ever raising her voice. She had that aura of quiet authority; she could simply ask people to be nice, play fair, and they almost always would. Partly, this authority seemed to come from her hat, a long-billed sun-protection job with a flap that hung down the back of her neck. There was something French Foreign Legion-ish about the hat, and it gave her the aspect of a long-enduring commander whose orders could not be questioned.

She was giving a lesson when Lenny walked up, so he stood just outside the court to watch. Sam waved, sang out a warm but brief hello, then turned her attention back to her paying customer.

The customer was tall, chesty, young, had too much make-up on, and looked like she had never before held a racquet in her life. Her sneakers looked brand new, the laces gleaming like tinsel in the sunshine. Her tennis dress still had the pucker from where that theft-proofing thingie had been cinched on. She didn't know where to stand. She didn't know the difference between a forehand and a backhand. Sam gently hit balls toward her and sometimes she whiffed altogether. Sometimes she hit grounders and sometimes she hit pop-ups. But what mostly struck Lenny about the woman was that she appeared undaunted and unembarrassed and seemed to be having a blast. She'd miss a shot and laugh. She'd arc one over the fence clear onto U.S. 1 and laugh again. Her laugh was distinctive and sparkling, starting with a faint pop that blossomed into something less staccato than a hoot, more delicate than a roar. It was impossible not to smile along.

When the lesson was over, the young woman took her brand new wristband off and said to Sam, "Oh my God, that was so much fun!"

Sam adjusted the bill of her Foreign Legion cap and said, "Yup, that's what it's supposed to be."

Almost skipping in her delight, the woman walked toward a bench where she'd left a big pink purse with black patent leather straps. This brought her close to where Lenny was standing, and bubbling over with enthusiasm, she gave him a quick smile that welcomed him into her monologue as she went on. "Me taking tennis lessons. That's a kick, right? But what took me so long? Actually, I know what took me so long. My mother. She tried to get me to do it. Years ago. Back in Queens. *Try tennis,* she'd say. *You'll meet a better classa people.* That kinda rubbed me wrong. I'd say, *better'n who? Better'n what?* So of course I didn't do it. Didn't practice piano either. Who was I spiting? Myself. As usual."

She hoisted the big pink purse onto her shoulder. Her eye make-up and dark lipstick were still in place after her workout and her long red fingernails seemed undamaged by their clench around the racquet. She said to Sam, "I just can't wait to do this again. Can we do it again tomorrow?"

Sam said, "Well, I'll have to check my book. How long are you in town for?"

At that, the young woman didn't exactly get cagey but her joyous and blithe enthusiasm seemed to dim just a little bit. "Not really sure. Sort of depends on my boyfriend. We're sort of playing things by ear right now."

"Ah," said Sam, who'd been in Key West long enough to know that a lot of people played a lot of things by ear and didn't always show up for lessons they'd booked. "Well, come into the shop a minute, we'll see what we can schedule."

Considerately, the young woman said to Lenny, "Hope I'm not cutting into your lesson time."

"Me? No, I'm just hanging out. Sam and me, we're old friends."

"You play together? You must be really good."

"No, I'm really average."

"Average would be a huge improvement. Well, gotta go. What's your name?"

"Lenny."

"I'm Carla. Hope to see you around the courts. That's what tennis players say, right?"

She turned and followed Sam toward the little pro shop.

"Christ, Peps," said Carmine, "why'dya have to volunteer us?"

They were sitting in a quiet bar on Broome Street, drinking Fernet-Branca, a miracle cure for indigestion and what they almost always drank after choking down a meal with Fat Lou.

"Why?" said Peppers. "How many reasons ya need? First of all, it's fuckin' winter here, in case you haven't noticed. Second, how often do we get an opportunity like this, a chance to get in on somethin' that might break big? Who knows, we get in good with this local guy, the Choo-Choo guy, maybe we got a future down in Florida."

"I hate Florida," Carmine groused.

"You hate Florida? You ever even been to Florida?"

"No I haven't. Why would I go? I hate it. Always onna news it's alligators, sinkholes, hurricanes, old Jews gettin' the wrong leg cut off in hospitals. Who needs that shit?"

Peppers fired down some Fernet, ran a hand through his hair until he realized he was in danger of mussing up the part that hid his bald spot. "Okay, you never been there 'cause you hate it. Very logical. Which brings me to the third reason I volunteered us to go down there. I volunteered us 'cause I'm hoping that a change of scenery might get you off this royal rag you're on and you'll stop being so knee-jerk grouchy negative about everything."

"Who's negative? I just got shit on my mind."

"Right. So what I'm sayin' is give it a rest. Let's go somewhere else, do something else, and maybe you'll stop bein' so goddamn grumpy."

Carmine finished off his *digestivo,* which really wasn't sitting that well on top of the *scungilli,* and gestured for another. "There's only one thing that's gonna make me stop bein' grumpy," he said, "and that's gonna be when this little douchebag comedian gets outta rehab so I can track him down and kill him. Until then, well, tough titty, I guess I'm gonna be a little grumpy."

"But how long?" said his buddy. "How long's he gonna be away? You don't know. You can't control it. Why make yourself miserable inna meantime?"

"I'm not miserable," the big man insisted. Neither of them believed it.

"Look, I'll cut you a deal," said Peppers. "We go to Florida. We get this ferry business done. You try at least to let go of this other bullshit. I'm guessing you will. In fact, I'm guessing you'll thank me for helping you get over this broad and sparing you the trouble of icing the comedian. But if it doesn't go that way, if you still feel like you need to whack the guy, I'll help you."

Rather sulkily, Carmine said, "Promise?"

"Promise."

"Okay, it's a deal."

8

While his new girlfriend was off taking a tennis lesson, Ricky Reed paced around their waterfront hotel room at the Harbor Inn and pondered the pickle he was in. Shacked up with a woman he liked a lot but had barely yet had time to get to know, and who had a former boyfriend whose picture you would see if you looked up sore loser in the dictionary. Not that anyone liked to have their girlfriend dump them and make it clear that they preferred another guy. But Carla's ex had taken his umbrage to maniacal extremes.

It had become clear early on that the failed Romeo was having her tailed. The surveillance soon discovered the midtown high-rise where Ricky lived. Then the stake-outs and the death threats had started. When a dead and stinking fish was dropped off with the doorman, Ricky decided this was no joke and that it would be best to get the hell out of town. He'd slipped out through a service alley, concocted the rehab story with the help of his agent, arranged for Carla to meet him at a car rental office in Weehawken, and headed south.

So here he was in Key West, pacing short laps between the bed and the *chaise*, looking out the window at boats bobbing in green water. It was actually pretty nice, except that he was running scared, hiding out. This was the exact opposite of what actors and comedians were supposed to do. They *appeared.* As in *Now appearing*...But he was now *dis*appearing. So everything—his life, career, reputation—was suddenly on hold. No doubt he'd disappointed lots of people who'd been working with him. Maybe he was missing his one and only chance to be a TV star. The lead role on *Groomer* would have been the perfect vehicle for him, assuming he could stay alive long enough to play the part. Instead, he was a fugitive.

This struck him as particularly unfair because, as far as he could remember at least, he hadn't gone out of his way to steal Carmine da Silva's girlfriend. She'd stolen herself. She'd made the first move. At least that's how Ricky remembered it. True, he didn't remember it that clearly.

He recalled that it started at a fancy club uptown, The Neapolitan, where they did cabaret, torch songs mostly, lots of comic patter thrown in between numbers to let the piano player rest his fingers. Ricky was at the bar with a couple of buddies. He'd had some pills and some vodka, then some different pills and some cognac, and his vision was a little glary and rounded at the edges, his hearing had a silvery sort of sheen to it. There'd be dues to pay for the high, there always were, but in the meantime he felt great and, comedy-wise, he was in that sweet zone where his mind was moving quicker than time itself, which meant that he could somehow anticipate what the next laugh line would be and the precise instant it would fall, and he could manage seamlessly to shim a wisecrack of his own into the cadence. He did this in an undertone mostly intended to be heard by the pals around him. He took the emcee's tepid witticisms and put a sharp edge on them. He improvised parodies of the song lyrics being sung. He was on a roll. Basically, he was just keeping himself amused.

But fate is fate, and it so happened that there was a table for eight set up within earshot of him. Four men, four women. They were drinking bottle after bottle of Cristal but they didn't seem to be having a whole lot of fun and they didn't quite seem to agree on what they were there for. Sometimes, like if the song was *Over the Rainbow,* it seemed like the women wanted to listen to the music but the men, elbows splayed wide, heads held low, were leaning across them deep in raspy conversation. Other times, like for instance if it was *My Way*, it seemed like the men wanted to hear the song but one of the women was in the middle of a story. So no one ended up really hearing much of anything.

They didn't laugh much at the patter either. Maybe the group just didn't think the stuff was funny, or maybe it was that the men thought it was undignified, a violation of their gravity, to drop their guard and get too cracked up in public, and maybe the women picked up a cue that if the men weren't laughing, they shouldn't laugh too damn much either. In any case, the eight of them just sat there drinking champagne and looking, at most, mildly amused or at least pleased with themselves for getting a good table at a fancy club.

Or seven of them sat that way. The one who didn't was tall and pretty and had originally been positioned so that her back was mostly to Ricky but she could sort of see him if she twisted to look over her left shoulder. She hadn't even noticed him when she'd first sat down, but as the evening went on she couldn't help overhearing his asides, his running commentary on the show, his quips. Humor just seemed to spurt out of him like a jet of water from a stony hillside, and the refreshment of it made the dry and plodding chitchat at her table seem even duller. By slow degrees, hoping that the movement would not be noticed, she pivoted just slightly in her chair, showing Ricky more of her profile, making the ear that was facing him the one that she was listening with.

Her companions at the table didn't seem to notice the attention-shift, but Ricky did. For him, it wasn't even a conscious noticing, just an entertainer's instinct to find what was working, find who it was working for, and play in that direction. So without exactly deciding to, he started, still in an undertone, playing to the tall woman with the big eyes and black hair. He sensed what she smiled at and what she didn't. On the fly, he was tailoring a routine to her reactions. Thing is, he wasn't flirting, he was riffing. At some point it became a lot like flirting, but that just sort of happened. It had never been the plan.

After a while the tall woman excused herself and got up to go to the ladies' room. Her path took her right past Ricky's barstool but she didn't linger for a schmooze. She understood her situation. She was the mistress of a very jealous guy who was not above making scenes at clubs. She wasn't supposed to talk to other men, she wasn't supposed to return their glances, and she knew that if she did, there would be trouble. So she just barely slackened her pace as she moved past Ricky and she said hardly above a whisper, "You're funny."

Ahead of the beat, quick as thought, he answered, "And you're beautiful. Wanna make something of it?" It wasn't a pickup line; well, it was, of course it was, though he didn't intend it that way at the time. It was just a comeback, a reflex, a morsel of improvisation.

She kept walking. He thought that was the end of it.

He couldn't know that, in the ladies' room, after she'd refreshed her makeup, Carla had taken a long look at herself. She was twenty-eight, which was almost twenty-nine, which was practically thirty, and she had a boyfriend who was clearly some kind of criminal, though she didn't know the details and didn't want to know them. Was this really what she wanted from her life? She was plenty smart enough to know there was no future in it. But forget the future. Was there even a present? True, there were some good times, nice places, nice things she couldn't have afforded on the wages she earned from her shifts at a cosmetics counter at Bloomingdale's. But there was also lots of boredom, lots of feeling like she was just tagging along on someone else's idea of what fun was, lots of feeling used. She was settling for too little and at honest moments she knew it. Standing there in front of the ladies' room mirror, shooting herself an I-dare-you kind of glance, she came to a bold and dangerous decision. She opened her purse, found a scrap of paper and an eyebrow pencil, then leaned down across the damp counter and wrote out her phone number.

She didn't look at Ricky when she sidled past him at the bar and slipped the paper into his hand. The contact between them was so quick and so light that he wasn't even sure if her fingertips had grazed his palm. He squeezed the unexpected and unread message and watched only casually as the tall woman reached her table, waited a futile moment for her date to pull her chair out for her, then pulled it out herself and resumed her seat among the group that wasn't laughing.

9

At Bayview Park, the slanting shadows were getting longer and the court surface was giving back the sunshine it had absorbed in the height of afternoon; waves of heat shimmered upward and tickled the players' legs.

Lenny, after hanging around the bleachers for a while and looking sort of lonely and pathetic, had finally been recruited into a doubles game with three of Bayview's regulars. One of them was wearing a diaper sort of get-up that wrapped around his loins and tied over one shoulder; he looked a great deal like Mahatma Gandhi would have looked if he ever wore high-top sneakers. Another kept a lit cigarette in his mouth and a spare behind his ear the whole time they were playing. The third resembled a *Gilligan's Island* castaway in flower-patterned clamdiggers and a polka-dot shirt with big buttons down the front.

They were deep into a set that was far from pretty but at least it was close. The score was 4-5 and the teams were changing ends when Lenny's phone rang.

He knew he shouldn't answer it in the middle of a match. He knew that, if he hoped to keep his focus, he shouldn't even look to see who was calling. But he did look, and when he saw it was his agent, Morty Feingold, he gave his court-mates an apologetic shrug and took the call. An out-of-work writer will always take the call.

"Morty," he said, trying to keep a naïve and needy hopefulness out of his voice, trying to sound like the unflappable veteran he wished he was, "what's up?"

"What's up? Nothing's up. Phone's not ringing. Just thought I'd check in, let you know I've been trying at least."

"Ah."

"Tough out there," said the agent, and Lenny could picture him saying it, sitting in his midtown office that always smelled of burnt coffee, pulling his heavy brows together, seeming to chomp on a phantom cigar even though he'd given up smoking years before. "Maybe tougher than I've ever seen it. But different tough. Ten years ago, problem was nobody wanted scripted shows. Everyone wanted reality bullshit. Now it's swung back, but there's too goddamn many writers."

"Some of them with agents who find gigs."

Morty let that pass. "They're flooding in like roaches. Guys who used to think TV was beneath them. Feature film guys, book guys. Suddenly everyone's got a series idea. Fuckin' irony is we were right there in the sweet spot with *Dog Groomer*. Right there in the sweet spot before we even knew it was the sweet spot. Damn shame it fell apart."

Lenny had put down his racquet, drifted away from his tennis partners, and was now clawing at the chain-link fence that ringed the court. Trying and failing to hold back the words, he said, "You think there'd still be interest?"

"You mean next year when Ricky's available? Who knows? Whole trend could be over by next year."

"No, I mean this year."

"Lenny, why even think about it? Why torment yourself? Our star wigged out and the schedule is the schedule."

"Morty, listen, I'm in Key West."

To the agent the segue made no sense. "So?"

"Staying with Pat Coates."

"Ah. You two cooking on a new idea? That's probably best. Forget this one and move on to something new."

"No, we're not working. I'm just sulking and brooding. On the outs with my wife."

Without undue sentimentality, the agent said, "Happens all the time. Classic."

"What? What's classic?"

"Writer hits the skids, gets bitter, self-esteem plummets, the marriage suffers. I'm sorry. Unless it was a shitty marriage to begin with. Then I'm not."

"It's not a shitty marriage," said Lenny, with a firmness and even defiance that surprised him. "It happens to be a terrific marriage. Mostly. But that's not what we were talking about. Morty, listen, are we in strict confidence here?"

"Of course we are. Who else gives a shit?"

"What would you say if I told you there's a pretty good chance that Ricky Reed isn't really in rehab and that he's here in Key West and that maybe, just maybe, we can get him to New York in time to shoot the pilot? What would you say?"

"I'd say you're delusional and should change your meds."

"And Pat? Is she delusional too? She's pretty sure she's seen him here in town and I'm starting to believe her."

"But why would he—?"

"Be here? Morty, I have no idea. I have no idea about anything. But in the meantime, do you think there'd still be interest for this year?"

"Yeah, I think there would be. The suits loved this thing."

"Can you please find out exactly how much time we have?"

"Without telling them anything? Without sounding like a lunatic?"

"Find a way, Morty. But listen, I gotta go. I'm in the middle of a very high-level tennis match. Practically the Open. Call me when you find out something, okay?"

He wandered back to the court. The other guys grumbled a bit about the delay but seemed to have kept their concentration. Lenny hadn't. On set point, a short lob came his way. He muffed the easy overhead and that was that. Everyone shook hands. The guy who smoked the whole way through had totally yellow fingers.

10

At the Paradiso condo, a complex of once deluxe, now outmoded buildings just across A1A from the green Atlantic Ocean, the old man Bert "the Shirt" d'Ambrosia was preparing his chihuahua's dinner. The process took a long time, and not only because Bert was a long-retired widower who needed to stretch out the routines with which he filled his days. It took a long time because the dog's dinner had to be prepared just so.

Not that the dog was finicky. It would've eaten and processed anything—raw hamburger, leftover broccoli, cheese ravioli straight from the can. But Bert was finicky on the dog's behalf. He wanted to believe that the dog was a connoisseur with a delicate digestion. So he measured out the kibble with a tablespoon and dosed out the water from a beaker. He put the mixture in the microwave for twenty-seven seconds, then he cut a half-inch slice from a gray and glutinous guts-and-rice loaf that promised to provide complete nutrition for dogs of all sizes and ages. He was just crumbling the greasy slice into the lukewarm kibble porridge when the old landline telephone on the kitchen wall started ringing.

This was very inconvenient and somewhat rattling, as Bert now had to deviate from his usual procedure and figure out what order things should be done in. There were problems either way. At Bert's age, it took a while to bend down while moving the dog's food from the counter to the floor; and of course it took him even longer to stand up again. So if he served the dog food first, he might miss the phone call, and a phone call was a pretty rare event in his life these days. If, on the other hand, he took the phone call and made the dog wait for its dinner, the dog would probably be miffed with him, plus the food would have to be reheated and the texture might come out all wrong. Precious seconds ticked away—the phone ringing, the dog quivering with excitement and staring with its bulging, glassy eyes—while Bert wrestled with his options. Finally, unable to decide, he reached for both the dog bowl and the phone at once.

This turned out to be a far from perfect solution, because the phone cord didn't stretch quite far enough for Bert to reach the little scrap of rug where the dog bowl needed to be placed. To make the geometry work, he had to set his feet wide apart, which cost him some of the leverage he would need for straightening up again. He also had to spread his arms as far as they could go, which somehow, as he swooped to bend, gave him the aspect of a minstrel singing *Mammy*. On top of that, his hands were greasy from the dog food loaf, and he had squeeze hard to keep the food bowl and the phone from slipping out of his grasp. In all, it called for a terrific effort, and by the time the old man was getting close to presenting the chihuahua's dinner while simultaneously rasping out a hello in the direction of the telephone mouthpiece, he was unconsciously grunting and a little out of breath.

A voice on the other end of the line said, "Christ, Bert, you okay? Ya sound like you're takin' a shit or somethin'."

"I'm not takin' a shit. I'm feedin' the dog. Who is this?"

"Who is it? It's Lou. Christ, Bert, you don't even recognize my voice no more?

"I'm kinda all stretched out here is the problem. Hol' onna a sec, lemme put the fucking dog bowl down before I rupture myself."

Carefully, he centered the bowl on the little mat that also held some water and a squeak toy. The chihuahua polished off the meal before its master had managed to get fully vertical again.

"Okay, Lou, that's better. So, to what do I owe the honor of hearing from you?"

"What, an old friend can't call an old friend just to say hello?"

"Yeah, an old friend can, but since an old friend hasn't in, oh, say the last fifteen years or so, I would tend to guess or let's say surmise that there is a motive for this phone call beyond the simple wish to renew acquaintances."

"Ah," said Luigi Benedetti, "same old Bert. Always suspicious."

He didn't deny it. He just waited for his former colleague to go on. While he waited, he pictured Fat Lou picking at his teeth, which he'd often seen him do in Brooklyn in the old days, even in the middle of a sitdown. It was a habit that Bert and a lot of other people found disgusting, but Lou was the boss and no one ever complained to him about it. He'd pick his teeth for hours after a meal. Sometimes it seemed like his whole fist was in his mouth when he went poking way back in the molars. But the worst part was that the toothpick would always come out with tiny bits of food on the end of it, and Lou would dab these samples—fractions of parsley leaves, fibers of veal, curls of tomato skin—onto a napkin in front of him. By the time he was through, the napkin would look like a miniature painting of the meal he'd most recently eaten.

Finally the New York boss went on. "Okay. Actually, I do have a small favor I'd like to ask."

"Big surprise. So ask it."

"I may be gettin' involved in a certain business arrangement down your way."

"Like what kinda business arrangement?"

"I'd rather not say for now."

"You'd rather not say, but I'm supposed to do you a favor anyway?"

"Yeah, that's pretty much it."

"Why would I do that?"

"Why?" said Benedetti, who may have had appalling table manners but was certainly no fool when it came to human nature. "Because you like to stick your nose in things. In fact, let's face it, Bert, you're about the nosiest sonofabitch I've ever known. No offense. You always were. I'm guessin' you're even more so now that you're retired and don't have much to do 'cept feed the dog."

"I manage to keep busy. In a Florida kinda way."

"Yeah, I bet your schedule's packed down there. Shuffleboard, gin rummy. S'okay, if you're too busy, no hard feelings. I just don't want ya to feel left out when the news breaks and you read it inna paper like all the other outsider nobodies, when ya coulda been someone who was in the know."

"Except I ain't in the know," Bert pointed out. "You ain't told me squat."

"Correct," Fat Lou admitted. Annoyingly, he said nothing more.

Bert wavered and got more curious. He hated to admit it, but Fat Lou had found his soft spot. "This business you might be gettin' into. 'Zit legal?"

"Up to a point."

"Anyone gonna get hurt?"

"I'm hoping not. Course, ya never know."

"Why here, Lou? Why Key West?"

"Joint venture. Well-connected local partner."

"Who?"

"You're out of questions, Bert. Will ya do this favor for me, yes or no?"

"What's the favor?"

Dropping his voice a notch, Benedetti said, "I'm sending a coupla guys down there. They're not what you might call the fluffiest pillows onna bed. But what can you do? The talent pool, it ain't like it was in the old days."

"I got news for ya," Bert put in. "It wasn't like it was in the old days in the old days either. I mean, come on, we didn't exactly have a buncha Einsteins."

Fat Lou let that slide. "Anyway, the one guy, name of Carmine, he's mainly for show. Muscle guy. Doesn't think. Better if he doesn't even try. But he's loyal."

"So's my dog. That doesn't mean I'd want him representin' me in a business matter."

Lou let that slide too. "The other guy, called Peppers, can think a little bit. Has some initiative. But a world-beater he's not."

"S'okay, you're sendin' these geniuses down. What is it you'd like me to do?"

"Ya know, just kinda show 'em the ropes, give 'em some local knowledge. Help 'em not fuck things up. Just kinda keep an eye on 'em."

"Keep an eye as in babysitting, or keep an eye as in spying for you?"

"Some a both. Ya know, keep me advised of their progress. Like I said, it's a favor. For you, maybe it's a front row seat on somethin' you might find interesting."

Bert looked down at his dog. The dog looked back at him through glassy eyes, then over at its food bowl as if it had no idea how the bowl had so quickly gotten empty. Bert knew he should say no to Lou. If he didn't say no, he'd be opening himself to aggravation and disruption and responsibility and maybe even violence; to all the things he'd told himself a dozen times he'd had enough of for a lifetime.

So he meant to say no; he really did.

What came out instead, was, "You got my number, Lou. Have your Abbott and Costello call me. I'll buy 'em a drink when they get to town. No promises beyond that."

PART TWO

11

"How's business, Doll?" said Ted Clifton as he lowered his prosperously spreading backside onto an empty stool, one of many, at Titters.

Pat Coates forced herself to smile at him. He had a smooth chubby face that was almost handsome except for the strangely pink eyelids and pale lashes that made his narrow and light-colored eyes look piggy. He wore expensive pants that bunched up on him anyway, and the sleeves of a powder-blue sweater were casually tied around his soft pink neck. Pat detested him, as did nearly everyone in Key West, though few people could afford to show it, given the extent of his business holdings and his reputation for petty revenges. She'd learned that smiling sweetly at Ted Clifton was probably the wisest tactic. Anything else would just egg him on.

Not that he seemed to need much encouragement to be annoying, insulting, and manipulative. It was actually impressive—almost charming, in a perverse sort of manner—how offensive he'd managed to be with a mere three words, spoken, as ever, in a calm and pseudo-friendly voice. He knew damn well that business was lousy; he knew damn well that Pat cringed at cutesy little endearments from men. He'd managed to needle her twice in one short sentence. Pat had to give him credit for economy, at least.

"Great. Fine. Terrific," she answered breezily. "What'cha drinking?"

He asked for a vodka martini with rocks and a twist, and while she was making it he looked around the place. He counted seven other customers thinly spread around a room that could seat maybe ninety or a hundred.

She delivered the drink, and he said, "Cheers. You know, I was just down on Duval Street. Sloppy's, Rick's—places were slammed."

"Well, it's early yet. What's it—barely seven? Entertainment doesn't start till nine."

"Yeah, same time as at Margaritaville. They were already packed, though."

"So glad to hear it. I was really worried Jimmy Buffett was running out of money."

He sipped his drink and she took the opportunity to slide away from him. His voice pursued her as she moved toward the sink and started to wash some glasses. "This place," he said. "You know why it isn't working? Why it'll never work? You're just too far from Duval."

"Am I?" she said, hanging the glasses upside down in their overhead racks. "Gee, Ted, I never noticed that. Then again, girls don't tend to be that good at geography."

"Half a *block* from Duval is too far," he said. "Half a block is death. You've seen how many places come and go there. The karaoke joint. The kebab place. Half a block. And you're, what, half a mile? How's anyone supposed to find you?"

"Some people do," she said.

He swiveled plumply on his stool and looked more closely at his fellow patrons. He guessed that a few of them were knuckleheads off the houseboats and the others were clueless tourists who didn't realize they hadn't reached downtown yet. He shrugged, rattled his ice, then, out of the blue, he said, "Your girlfriend. She subsidizing this place?"

"That's none of your business."

"I see her out on the court all hours. Works her tail off. Can't be easy. Broiling sun. So much skin cancer going around. Basal cell. Melanoma. Hate to think she's doing all that to support a place that just can't work."

"The place pays for itself," said Pat. "Almost."

"You signed a lousy lease. Too long. Too much money for such a crummy spot."

Pat picked up a rag and started dusting bottles on the back bar. The bottles weren't dusty but she preferred keeping busy to giving Ted her full attention and getting angry. "Do we really need to go through this again?" she said. "It's not a great lease. I know that. I committed to it and I'm going to see it through."

"Foolish," he said. "When you could sell it to me, get out from under, come away with a few bucks even, and be free to spend these balmy romantic evenings with your pretty tennis teacher."

She stopped dusting and put the cloth down. She said, "Ted, enough about my pretty tennis teacher. And if it's such a bad lease and such a bad location, why are you so hot to buy it from me?"

"Why? Simple. Because I can make it work in a way you can't. Any time I like, I can re-route the Choo-Choo so it stops right at the gangplank. I can bring hundreds of people right here every day and every night."

Pat bit her lip. The thought of doing business with Ted Clifton was extremely distasteful, and the thought of asking him for a favor was even more so. Still, the notion of an endless stream of customers being delivered right to the door...Quietly, she said, "If you wanted to, you could do that anyway. Re-route the train, I mean. I'd pay you a cut."

He smiled at that and gave a flick to the tied arms of his sweater. "Everybody pays me. That's understood. But why would I do that when I want the place for myself?"

Abashed, feeling soiled that she'd even tentatively offered to pow-wow with this bully, Pat didn't bother masking her sarcasm. "Ah, I just thought that since you rooted so sincerely for my success—"

"Did I say that?" Clifton interrupted, as he started backing almost daintily off his barstool. "I don't think I ever said I was hoping you'd succeed. I just said it was a shame you're failing."

Standing now, he drained his drink and dropped a twenty on the bar. Pat looked at it as if it had birdshit on it, then used a fingernail to push it back toward him. "On the house," she said.

He smiled sourly. "Ah, the grand gesture. Just the kind of thing you can't afford."

He tried waiting her out. They both looked at the money. She didn't reach for it. Finally he picked up the bill and stuffed it into the pocket of his expensive but rumpled pants. "Stubborn," he said, with a twist of his very pink neck. "Extremely stubborn."

12

When Carla, still glowing from the sheer and simple fun of her tennis lesson, got back to her room at the Harbor Inn, she found Ricky jumping up and down on the bed, playing air guitar. He was wearing a loosely belted hotel bathrobe that he'd sultrily shrugged off one shoulder and he had a washcloth on his head in place of a do-rag. Gyrating, twanging at strings that weren't there, eyes squeezed so tightly shut that he felt his whole scalp move, he welcomed her home with some raspy improvised rap.

"Honey, I got this pow'ful craving.

Felt it first while I was shaving.

Swelled up right there in the shower,

Been jonesin' bad for a long, tough hour.

Devil tempted me to reach for pills,

Angel said No, man, wait for thrills.

Uppers, downers, they're a hex.

Fuck that rehab, heal with sex.

So don't deny me, be my nurse,

Lose that upper-downer curse.

Love me morning, noon, and night,

Chase the demons, make me right."

She put down her racquet and the big pink purse with the patent leather straps, and looked up at him standing on the bed, flushed but very still now in the twisted and tormented robe. His eyes had fallen open; the look in them was boyish, almost shy.

She said, "Now?"

He took the washcloth off his head, dropped the rasp and the hip-hop cadence, and spoke in his own real voice, a voice he didn't use as often as he might have. "Yeah, now," he said. "Please? I really need to have your arms around me. Please?"

⛱ ⛱ ⛱

Later, over a room service dinner of conch fritters and steamed lobster, Carla said to him, "Ricky, this hiding out, this paranoia, are we maybe taking it a little bit too far?"

"Paranoia?" he answered. "Paranoia is like when you imagine that tiny people are putting bombs in your cereal to blow up your teeth. I don't think it's paranoia when someone with a grudge comes right out and says he's gonna rip your heart out. When he hands a dead fish to your doorman."

"Okay, bad choice of words." She'd been nibbling a conch fritter. The outside of it was very crispy and left behind a few delicious crumbs in the striations of her lips. She dabbed them daintily away. "So it isn't paranoia. But Carmine's fifteen hundred miles away. Don't you think it's safe to go out of the hotel, at least? I mean, without being naked and wearing a fright wig and glasses that Elton John might've had in 1982?"

"There was a reason for that," he said. "I was reaching out to my old friend Pat. She's smart. Maybe she could help me out somehow."

"Fine, I get it. But I've kind of been wondering: You couldn't call her on the phone?"

Somewhat sheepishly, he said, "I guess I could have. Yeah. But where's the impact in that? I wanted it to have some impact. Besides, I was a little hopped up and it was fun."

"Fun," she echoed, sipping some wine. "And don'tcha think it might be fun to see some daylight now and then? Go to the beach? Do some sightseeing? You know, leave our little love nest long enough for them to change the sheets?"

He dipped a chunk of lobster into butter sauce before he answered. "And what if I get recognized?"

The question put Carla in an uncomfortable position because it raised the issue of just how famous Ricky was, as opposed to how famous he liked to think he was. Was Ricky Reed a household name? No. Had he been the star of anything big? No, not so far. Did paparazzi follow him around? Absolutely not. This relative obscurity might save his life, but that didn't mean he wanted to be reminded of it. He was a performer, after all; he had his vanity.

So Carla kept a tactful silence, but Ricky must have picked up on something skeptical in her expression, because he pointed at her with his little lobster fork and said, "It would just take one, you know. One fan sees me, throws a photo onto Instagram. Carmine sees it, he knows where I am, boom, I got all kinds of trouble."

"Carmine's not exactly a social media kind of guy," said his former girlfriend. "I mean, what's he gonna post? *Here I am in Little Italy. I'm eating meatballs.* Can you even imagine him tapping out a post with those gigantic thumbs?"

"I don't really need to hear about your old flame's gigantic thumbs or any of his other digits either. But okay. Tell you what—tomorrow we'll go out. We'll do something. Anything you like. Just think about it, what you'd like to do."

"I already know what I'd like to do," she said. "I've been thinking about it all evening."

"All evening?"

"Well, not when we were making love." This was a slight but necessary fib. "All evening except for that."

"And what is it that you'd like to do?"

"I'd like us to go together to that funny little park and hit some tennis balls."

13

It was around midnight when Peppers and Carmine crossed the St. Marys River and entered Florida, and the big man behind the wheel started grousing at once about the state.

"Shit," he said, "it ain't even warm here. Dashboard thing says forty-four."

"Wasn't warm two minutes ago in Georgia either," Peppers pointed out. "Ya think they throw a switch?"

"Bein' hot," said Carmine, "that's like the one thing the fuckin' place has goin' for it, and even that turns out to be bullshit."

"The hot part," Peppers pointed out, "that's like five hundred miles from here."

"Five hundred miles? The fuckin' state goes on five hundred miles?"

"Long state. Plus then ya got the Keys."

They drove in silence for a while. Carmine scanned the road ahead and the marshes off to either side and shook his head like everything he saw was a personal affront. "Christ, it's flat."

"And what's New York, the fuckin' Alps?"

"New York don't feel flat. There's buildings. Ya got, whaddyacallit, shapes. There's some, I dunno, up and down. Here there's nothing but fuckin' sideways. Five hundred miles of fuckin' sideways."

Peppers saw no point in arguing. He looked out the window.

A few miles later he said, "Here's somethin' that might cheer you up a little bit. Know the first thing we're gonna do when we hit Key West?"

"Yeah. Get a hotel room, take a dump, and get some fuckin' sleep."

"And first thing after that?" his buddy soldiered on. "We're gonna have a drink with a living legend. Ever hear of a guy named Bert the Shirt?"

"Not really."

"Whaddya mean, not really? Either ya heard of someone or ya didn't. Anyway, this Bert d'Ambrosia used to be *consigliere* to the Peretti family. Tough bastard when he had to be, but more known as a peacemaker. Got people to talk to each other, work things out. Was really helpful to Fat Lou when Lou was coming up. Lou admits it. Says Bert was kind of a mentor to him."

"Mentor?" Carmine said. "So that means he's even older than Lou? Christ, what are we, the Mafia or a fuckin' nursing home?"

"Negative, negative, you're always negative," said Peppers. "So happens the guy sounded very sharp on the phone. And however old he is, he must have at least a little juice left in him, 'cause he asked us to meet him nine o'clock tomorrow night at a strip club."

"Strip club?" Carmine said, and for the first time since the Holland Tunnel, he came close, though not that close, to smiling.

"That sounds a little better, right?" said Peppers. "See some skin, catch a little lap dance action maybe?"

It sounded damn good in the midst of the long and boring drive, but Carmine wasn't willing to come right out and admit it. "Strippers are prob'ly, like, ninety. Prob'ly need walkers to get over to the pole. Prob'ly give one last twerk and keel over."

"All right, stay negative," Peppers said with a shrug, and decided he'd just go back to looking out the window.

They were already skirting Jacksonville by the time he spoke again. "Least I think it's a strip club," he resumed. "I mean, it must be. Name like that, what else could it be? Titters. Gotta be a strip club, right?"

⚓ ⚓ ⚓

Pat was wiping down tables with an evil-smelling solution of ammonia and vinegar. Lenny was mopping the floor with a bad mop whose strands kept catching in the gaps between the floorboards. Mopping wasn't something he was good at, and he felt that he was mainly just chasing hair-balls from one corner to another. It was one-thirty in the morning.

"Ah, show business," he said, bending low to pick up a recalcitrant glob of oily dust. "The glitz. The glamour."

"That's what people think, right?" said Pat. "Think it's all red carpets, klieg lights, and appearances on *Late Night*. No one thinks about who stacks the chairs."

"Ever think of quitting?"

"Sure. Every night around this time. Doesn't everybody think of quitting when they're tired?"

She wiped down another table. Lenny chased hair balls some more. By way of consolation, he said, "Well, there were some funny bits tonight. Like that guy with the parrot on his shoulder. Except there wasn't any parrot. He just made you believe there was. The way he looked at it, talked to it. The whole audience started seeing this non-existent bird."

Wearily, Pat said, "And I guess that's why I'm still doing this. So an audience can laugh at a bird that isn't there. I mean, that could only happen live, right? It's just different from someone chuckling over a book or laughing at TV. Strangers laughing together at something right in front of them. It's just different."

"Yeah, it is."

Pat threw down her rag, stood up tall, and arched her back. "And I happen to believe there's value in it."

Lenny said, "Who's arguing?"

"Guess I'm arguing with myself." She shrugged and pumped some more ammonia spray. "A guy came in today. Wants to buy out my lease. If he wasn't such a creep and bully I'd be half-tempted."

Lenny said nothing. He wasn't doing such a fabulous job of running his own life; he didn't feel like he should say much about how friends ran theirs.

His silence didn't matter. Pat, tired as she was, now brought a certain fury to the wiping of the tables. "But fuck it," she went on, "I won't do it. Look, there's fifty, sixty places in this town that have live entertainment. As in music. How many feature live comedy? One. This one. I cave, what happens to the make-believe parrot?"

"He's toast," said Lenny. "But don't worry, you won't cave."

"You sound pretty sure of that."

"I am. I've known you a long time." He leaned on the mop and continued chasing dust into the corners of the room.

14

Lenny formed habits easily. The next day, he again had an afternoon nap and when he woke up it just felt like it was time to head to the park and look for some tennis. He pulled on the borrowed shorts, grabbed Pat's racquet that had already gotten to feel familiar in his hand, and headed down the same shady streets as on the day before toward Bayview.

But he hadn't yet reached that stage of habit when even the things one looks at have become habitual, so he noticed different things this time. Window-shutters, for example. It was amazing the way window-shutters defined the personalities of Key West houses. They came in colors like gelato. Lemon-lime, raspberry, blueberry, pistachio. Some were plumb and almost too tidy, others sagged and slouched as if in surrender to the torpor of the almost-tropics. Some made grand statements with little heart shapes cut into the wood, or silhouettes of pineapples, the emblem of hospitality. He also noticed how the shifting patterns of dappled sun and shade seemed to leave a kind of stencil on his skin; where sunshine landed even for a moment, a prickle of delicious heat was felt. He was at that stage of gratitude and wonder—generally it lasted a week or so—when visitors didn't yet take the sunshine and the warmth for granted. He was still surprised not to be cold in January.

At the courts, many of the same knuckleheads were playing in various configurations. Lenny took a seat in the bleachers and waited for an opening in a foursome. While he was waiting, he noticed, three courts away, the pretty, chatty woman who'd taken her very first lesson the day before. Today she was hitting with a partner. Or trying to. The partner was about as bad as she was.

He was an average-size guy with heavily tattooed arms, a thick black beard that carpeted his face all the way to the cheekbones, and a long-billed baseball cap pulled low across his eyes. He seemed to like hitting the ball really hard and a lot of his shots pinged off the fence. When that happened, the tall brunette would laugh; the partner would put his hands on his hips in mock disgust, then he'd laugh too.

Finally he launched one clear out of the enclosure. It rolled almost to the softball field beyond. Lenny got up from the bleachers and went to retrieve it for them. He brought it close to the fence so he could toss it over, then, from behind the windscreen said, "Hey Carla, here you go."

She looked up and squinted through the mesh of the screen. "Oh, hi. Lenny, right? Thanks a lot."

"You're welcome. Glad you found someone to hit with."

Carla hesitated. She didn't know much about the etiquette of tennis courts but she figured if Lenny had been nice enough to fetch the ball for them, then she should at least introduce her partner. She said, "Oh, yeah, this is my boyfriend, um, Tom. Tom."

"Hi, Tom-Tom," Lenny shouted out. From the tattooed man's perspective, the other was just a shape behind the screen.

"Hi-hi," he answered.

That was the whole exchange. The partner's eyes had never lifted beyond the shadow of the cap. The two brief syllables had issued forth from a mere hole in the beard. Even so, there was a vague something in the fleeting contact that nagged at Lenny, something faintly familiar but unplaceable. Something in the fellow's posture? The timbre of his voice? It was probably nothing, just a symptom of being in a strange town where everyone vaguely reminded him of someone else. He went back to the bleachers.

A couple of minutes later it was Carla's turn to hit a homer. Hers landed on US 1, where it was deflected by a passing rent-a-car that sent it rolling just to the edge of a sewer grate. Dutifully, Lenny went to grab it.

From the street side of the fence he called out, "Hey Tom-Tom, here you go."

"Thanks-thanks," the other man said. They were standing a mere three feet apart by then, the windscreen between them blurring but not opaque.

Lenny said, "Sorry, but I keep feeling like I know you from somewhere."

That seemed to make the partner nervous. He tugged his cap still lower and spoke into his chin. "No-no. I don't think so."

"New York maybe?"

"Never been there. Never."

"Okay-okay. My mistake." He started to walk back toward the park entrance.

Carla's partner waited till he'd moved away a step or two, then bent low to sneak a look at him from underneath the level of the windscreen. He hesitated a heartbeat more before bounding close and pressing his shoulder against the fence. "Hey, wait a second," he said in a hissing whisper. "Holy crap. Lenny? Lenny Sullivan? What the fuck you doing here?"

"Ricky? Ricky Reed? What the fuck *you* doing here? You're supposed to be in rehab."

"I am. Kind of."

"What's with the tats?"

"Stick-ons."

"And the beard?"

"Ditto. Basic little disguises. I brought along a suitcase-full. Been feeling kind of paranoid."

"So the naked bit at the club the other night. That was really you?"

"Who else could it have been? I killed, right?"

"I don't know. I wasn't there. But you still haven't told me why the hell you're in Key West."

Ricky got a little cagey then. "You haven't told me either."

At that, Lenny quickly crossed over from curiosity to exasperation, and from exasperation to a blame he hadn't quite let himself admit before. "Why am I here? Okay, I'll tell you why I'm here. I'm here because I walked out on my wife because we couldn't stop arguing, and it's partly your fault."

"My fault? Wha'd I do?"

"You screwed us. You bolted on our pilot, which left me without a job or any prospects, which made me kind of mopey and pathetic, which made my wife start picking on me, which made me really touchy and defensive until I bailed, and now it turns out that your whole story was bullshit, you're not in rehab, you're streaking clubs and wearing lame disguises and dicking around on a tennis court like some crazy, selfish—"

"Lenny, someone wants to kill me. That's why I'm here."

Traffic was going by on US 1. There were cars, trucks, scooters. The windscreen between the two men's faces swallowed up some of the sound of their voices. Lenny said, "What?"

He said it again.

"You serious?"

"Serious as a nuke attack. Sorry about your marriage."

"But wait a second. Who would want—"

"Carla's former boyfriend. Mafia. I think they call it a vendetta. Which I think is Italian for you're fucked."

"Holy shit."

"My feelings exactly."

"Have you tried calling the po—"

Lenny didn't get to finish the sentence, because just then a guy screamed out from the bleachers. "Hey, people are waitin' to play tennis here. You two gonna parlez-vous all day?"

By a New York reflex, Ricky yelled back, "Yeah, probably. And screw you too."

"Fuckin' tourist!"

"Fuckin' yahoo local!"

Lenny said, "Ricky, um, we don't want to get on the wrong side of the pro here. Why don't we continue this at Pat's?"

15

"Feel better now?" asked Peppers Carlucci, as Carmine emerged from the bathroom of their oceanfront mini-suite at the Flagler House hotel.

"Better'n what?" the big man sourly asked, then threw himself down on one of the neatly made queen beds.

Peppers had pulled back the curtains and was looking out the fourth floor window at the still water of the Florida Straits. Close to shore it was a milky green, almost soupy, but the sand soon sifted out of it, leaving a swath of emerald that grew gradually less transparent as it deepened. The sky was mostly clear except for a few distant and cottony clouds tinged that exact same green on their bottoms. Gesturing like a game-show emcee showing off a prize, he said, "Will you look at that? How can you still be bitching with a view like that?"

"Water's flat," groused Carmine. "Everything in this fuckin' state is flat. Even the ocean. I like waves."

"An' if there was waves, you'd prob'ly say you like it flat."

"Yeah, prob'ly."

Peppers sighed and sat down on the bed that by default had become his. Thoughtfully, deliberately, he wrestled off his shoes and sniffed his nylon socks. They were crusty after the long drive and they stank. He rolled them into a ball and threw them in the garbage. Then he said, "Carmine, you ever worry that your lousy attitude is gonna hold you back in life?"

"That's a good one. Hold me back from what?"

"Oh, I dunno. New opportunities. I mean, 'zis what you wanna be doin' when you're fifty, sixty? Intimidating people? Breaking arms? Running bosses' errands?"

"I'll be a boss by then," said Carmine, though he fell a bit short of mustering the bravado that such a statement called for. "I won't be doin' this shit for people. People'll be doin' it for me."

Peppers was examining his toes. There were dry white cracks between the two littlest ones and they itched like crazy. Shaking his head very slowly, he said, "No offense, Carmine, but you ain't gonna be a boss. I ain't gonna be a boss either. Know why? 'Cause to be a boss, there's gotta be something to be boss *of,* and let's face it, what you and me might get the chance to be boss of has been gettin' its ass kicked for years and years already. There's gonna be fuck-all left by the time our turn comes around."

Carmine half-turned on his side to face his buddy. He badly wanted to disagree with the assessment of their prospects but couldn't find the words or the conviction. Instead, he said, "Listen who's bellyachin' now. Mister positive. Mister cheerful."

"I'm not bellyachin'. I'm bein' realistic."

"Why's it bellyachin' when I do it and bein' realistic when you do it?"

"I'm thinkin' about our future," Peppers said. "I'm just sayin' maybe there's something better for us out there."

Carmine gestured vaguely toward the window. "Out there. Out where? Inna fucking sky?"

"I don't know out where, okay? But away from New York maybe. Away from the social club and the meatballs and the heartburn and the aggravation. Someplace new. Maybe even right down here in Florida. "

"I hate Florida."

"I picked up on that. But all you done since you been here is sit inna car, make a number two, and now you're layin' onna bed. You haven't exactly opened yourself to the experience."

"No, and I'm not gonna open myself to squat until a certain unfinished piece a business is taken care of."

"Christ, still with the hard-on about the comedian?"

"Damn straight."

"Okay, okay. But can we please look beyond that for a second? Like, at the big picture? This job, this ferry thing, this local bigshot. We handle things right, maybe it's a once-in-a-lifetime opportunity."

"Maybe it's a big pain in my ass."

"Maybe it will be. But can we please keep an open mind, at least? And maybe, ya know, try to, like, ingratiate ourselves."

"*Ingratiate* ourselves? Fuck's that mean?"

"Like maybe, for starters, try to smile now and then. A little bit, at least. Ya think you can do that, Carmine? Ya think you could smile a little bit?"

The big man gave it a grudging try. It took several separate twitches to jerk his lips back from his teeth, as if his lips were worked by rusty cables wound through balky gears.

Peppers looked at the resulting snarl and said, "Okay, maybe it's better if you don't."

Carmine turned over and put a pillow on his head.

16

"So my personal, unofficial rehab thing," Ricky Reed was saying. "I guess you could say I've been trying the love cure."

"Or the sex cure," Carla put in.

"I was trying to be delicate."

"Hey, I'm from Queens. Besides, it's nice to feel I'm helping."

They were sitting over beers in Pat's small but perfect backyard. The pool pump hummed, wind whispered in the shrubbery. Ricky still had the fake tats all up and down his arms, but now that he'd found himself among friends, he'd pulled off the black beard; the backing left some fuzzy lint behind on his otherwise smooth cheeks. The beard itself, tossed onto the table, looked either like roadkill or a disembodied pubic bush.

"Totally unscientific approach," Ricky explained. "Not saying it would work for everyone. And I'm not saying I've totally sworn off pills. I happen to enjoy them. Just saying I'm doing a way better job of holding it together, keeping things under control." As a bit of an afterthought, he added, "And yeah, Carla's really been a help."

In the earnest but inevitably stiff way that people generally respond to someone else's good news, Lenny said, "That's great. That's really great."

"Fabulous," said Pat.

Then there was a brief dead spot in the conversation as the two old friends shared a private glance, each hoping the other would take the lead in sliding the conversation away from Ricky's problems and Ricky's sex life and toward the practical business of seeing if they could possibly get their TV pilot back on track. Rather chickenheartedly, Lenny stalled by sipping his beer. Pat cleared her throat and said, "Well, Ricky, since you're doing so much better, I was wondering if—"

"We could head up north and shoot?" said the presumptive lead in *Dog Groomer to the Stars*. He shook his head with a mix of sorrow, frustration, and temperamental swagger. "I'm sorry. Super sorry. For myself, mainly. I mean, I've really wanted this. Big leap for me. But it's not worth getting killed about, and if I go back to New York, I'll probably get killed."

Carefully, Lenny said, "Ricky, do you think there's any chance you're exaggerating the danger maybe just a little bit?"

"He isn't," Carla said quietly but in a tone that left no doubt. "I know the man. He'd do it."

"Have you spoken to the police?" asked Pat.

"What're they gonna do?" said Ricky. "Guard me 24/7 just because I ask them to? Just because I tell them someone's really mad at me?"

"Maybe get some kind of restraining order?" Lenny offered.

"Right. What're my grounds? That he once gave a fish to my doorman? A judge is gonna start handing out restraining orders every time some guy delivers seafood? Pizza? Take-out Thai? I don't see it happening."

The pool skimmer gurgled. People sipped their beers. Pat said, "Maybe the jealous lover bit'll just die down."

"Not likely," said Carla. "I mean, all in all Carmine's got the attention span of a hamster. Except when it comes to grudges."

Pat drummed fingers on the little table and turned to Lenny. "Do we know the drop-dead date for starting to film?"

"Hey, talk about insensitive," said Ricky.

Lenny said, "Not sure. Morty's trying to find out. I'm guessing we have a week or so."

The would-be star hung his head theatrically. "Can't happen. It's a shame, but there's no way."

Carla moved to rub the back of his hand. He was feeling twitchy just then and he pulled it off the table.

Pat said, "Oh well. There's always next season."

Lenny finally gave in to a spasm of gloom. "And we'll be soiled goods by then. Expired yogurt at the supermarket. Okay, so it goes."

There was a silence. Pat stood up. "Well, in the meantime I've got a club to run and I need to get ready. Why don't you all come down later and see the show? Might be worth a couple laughs. I think we all could use a couple."

Carla brightened at once. Ricky didn't. She said, "Come on, wouldn't it be nice to get out, hang around with people?"

"I dunno. Out in public—"

"Public? Honey, really. We're in Key West with friends. Carmine's fifteen hundred miles away. You've got plenty more disguises if you really think you need one. I mean really, what's the harm?"

⚓ ⚓ ⚓

It was a rare event when Bert d'Ambrosia got visitors from The City, or visitors from anywhere in recent years, and so he made a point of dressing for the occasion.

Standing in his closet amid the rich and comfortingly familiar smells of moth balls, dry cleaning fluid, residue of Old Spice, and mildew, he riffled through a rack of shirts in linen and in silk, in solids and bold patterns, brooding deep hues and pastels. He wanted something appropriate for a casual first-time chat with a couple of New York wiseguys, or at least a couple of New York wiseguys as they might have dressed in nineteen sixty-eight. At length he selected a classic cotton white-on-white with a narrow placket, French cuffs, and a collar about as wide as a 747. For cufflinks, he chose a pair that were made to look like dice, and whose geometry went well with the offset squares in the embossing of the shirt. Since it was January and the comedy club was often drafty, he also pulled on an alpaca vest, exactly the kind that Perry Como used to wear, in fire-engine red.

Then it was time to dress the dog.

He preferred to dress the dog in a matching outfit whenever possible, but since he'd never seen an embossed dress shirt with four sleeves in the size of a chihuahua, he had to settle for a snug wool jacket in the same emphatic red as his vest. To echo the cufflinks, just in case anybody noticed, he snapped a pair of plastic dice onto the dog's collar as an accent.

Then he left his condo and began the slow and shuffling walk across Bertha Street toward Garrison Bight. He felt pretty good about how he'd be spending the evening. He enjoyed doing favors for people, and this evening he'd be helping out a few different people at once. Doing a solid for an old colleague from the glory days. Giving some advice and guidance to a couple of young goombahs who knew squat about the local turf. Best of all, he'd be spending some money and bringing some warm bodies into Titters, a place he rooted for and which was not exactly thriving.

And, of course, along the way he'd be indulging his curiosity, not to say nosiness, about what Fat Lou was after in Key West, this purported big deal that was brewing. So, as far as Bert could tell, it was a win, win, win, and win. He was, at least for one more precious evening, in the middle of something, involved in the younger world around him. He was bringing people together, sharing what he knew, helping out his friends. It was the kind of thing he lived for.

17

It was almost eight p.m. when Marsha returned from the New Jersey college where she taught and stepped into the rather threadbare apartment on the stubbornly ungentrified block of the Upper West Side. As she was placing her heavy books on the small oak table in the foyer, the door clicked shut behind her with the particularly dry, hard, unfriendly sound that doors make when there is no one else at home. She hung up her coat in the entryway closet. It rubbed up against Lenny's coat—the one she hadn't reminded him to put on when he went to move the car and ended up fleeing to Key West instead—in a kind of ghostly caress.

She saw his coat hanging there and she missed him. She couldn't deny it, and she didn't want to deny it. All she wanted was to understand what had gone wrong and to figure out if it could be made right again.

It was true that Lenny had been awfully difficult lately, relentlessly glum behind the wisecracks, touchy and fragile behind the wall of jokes. But it was also true that she'd been pretty tough on him. Her criticizing came from love—and, okay, from frustration—and it was meant to help, to nudge him out of the rut he was in. Except he didn't seem to see it that way; and, in fairness, she had to admit that she hadn't always been as gentle or as tactful as she might have been. But hell, she wasn't having the easiest time either. What thinking person was these days?

Wrapped up in this tangle of thoughts, she went to the kitchen and rummaged through the fridge for some leftovers to reheat. As soon as they were in the microwave she poured herself a glass of wine and gave in to earnest but unhelpful ponderings about the state of the world. It was a disheartening mess and it was putting millions of people into many different shades of rotten mood; but had she and Lenny really been letting it screw up their marriage? Why? Because she vented her outrage by going to marches and he vented his by making subversive jokes? It was the same outrage either way. It should have brought them closer together, not driven them apart.

She paused in her thinking and saw that her wineglass was empty. Until then, she hadn't exactly noticed that she'd been drinking the wine, and this made her feel that she'd somehow been cheated out of the first glass. She poured herself some more and continued mulling. Her and Lenny's differences—weren't they really more about style than substance? When she had something to say, she said it by way of logical argument; Lenny's method was the sudden comic ambush. Was it really fair to say that her way was serious and his just wasn't?

The microwave dinged.

She reached in, grabbed a bowl of steaming but somewhat dried out rigatoni, and carried it over to the scratched-up kitchen table. She ate a few forkfuls but soon decided that the food held less interest than the wine. She kept thinking about Lenny's implacably, undauntedly, relentlessly cockeyed approach to things, and she had to smile to herself. She'd always loved that about him. So why had it been grating on her lately? Because he'd had a bad break and was out of work? Because a dangerous clown was President and people like her were finding it harder to laugh, or harder to laugh without feeling guilty? Was that Lenny's fault? Besides, it's not as if he was about to change. He couldn't. Wisecracks were like a part of his religion, his way of making sense of things, peace with things.

She polished off her second glass and poured herself a third. She usually didn't drink much and she pretended not to know why she was doing so now, but in her heart she did. She was drinking to give herself a brief vacation from her logic and analysis, an excuse to drop the A student routine and go slumming through the middlebrow emotions like sentiment and nostalgia. She found herself reflecting on some of the things she loved about being with Lenny. The yeasty smell of his side of the bed. The almost fanatical concentration he brought to simple tasks like flipping an omelet or shaving underneath his nostrils. His loyalty to inanimate objects—coffee cups, sweaters, or like the way he'd get attached to a particular toothbrush and use it till the bristles were all splayed out. Silly things. Trivial things. Probably irreplaceable. Irreplaceable! As in *gone forever?* That was a brutal and terrifying concept, and it threatened to push her beyond the sentimental and toward the maudlin.

She poured some more wine and was surprised to find that it was the end of the bottle. As she sipped it, a new kind of fierceness gradually took hold of her and seared away the mawkishness. She decided that she simply wasn't going to let her marriage end, certainly not over a pointless argument about who was serious and who was not. That would be a terrible waste and she wasn't going to let it happen. She was going to fix things. She was going to win her husband back.

But how? She drummed her fingers on the table and tried to think of a tactic, an opening move, at least. She could apologize for her part in their recent tiff, and that would probably help, but on its own it seemed inadequate and a little pale. She wanted something more resonant, more immediate, something that would really show him she was trying to reconnect, find common ground, start fresh.

At length she felt she'd found the perfect way. With most of a bottle of wine in her mostly empty stomach, it struck her as an excellent idea. Uncharacteristically, she even giggled to herself about it. Fumbling around in the bottom of her purse, she found her phone and called him up.

He answered on the third ring. His hello sounded a little rushed or harried, which unsettled her but not to the point of undoing her resolve. Without hesitation or greeting, she said, "So a rabbi, a horse, and a midget walk into a bar..."

He said, "Marsha? Is this you? Your voice is kind of slurry."

"...And the bartender, who's Polish, says—"

"Are you drunk, Marsha?"

"No, wait. It's the midget who's Polish—"

"You sound pretty drunk. Are you schnockered?"

She hesitated then said, "A little. I guess." Quite suddenly, her great idea no longer seemed so great and her voice got small and sheepish. "I wanted to tell you a joke."

"That's nice. That's really nice. But listen, I don't have time for jokes right now."

"But you love jokes. You always have time for jokes."

"Not at the moment. Things have gotten kind of serious down here."

The unexpected word sobered her up a bit, but it also confused her and her answer came a fraction after the beat. "Serious? Did you say serious? When I'm finally trying to be funny?"

"Ricky Reed's down here. Someone wants to kill him."

The news came totally out of nowhere and would have been utterly bewildering even without the wine. She just said, "What?"

"His new girlfriend's old boyfriend."

"New...girlfriend's...old...boyfriend," she repeated, enunciating carefully as she tried to follow the convoluted phrase.

"He's Mafia."

"Mafia? Are you serious?"

"I just said I was. But listen, Marsha, I gotta go. I'm picking them up at their hotel."

"Picking who up? The Mafia?"

"Ricky. Ricky and the new girlfriend."

"You just said someone wants to kill him. I don't think you should pick him up."

"It's okay, Marsha. The guy's in New York. But in the meantime, me and Pat, we have to help Ricky figure out a way to stay alive."

"Maybe that's more Ricky's problem."

"It's our problem too. Lots of reasons. He's a good guy. Little fucked up but means well. Can't not help. Plus, if we get things straightened out, maybe there's even still a chance of doing the show."

"Who cares about the show? Lenny, this is Mafia, people getting killed maybe."

"I'd have work again. Maybe make a lot of money."

"I don't care about the money. I care about you. Please, Lenny, you be very careful. I love you."

She hadn't expected to say those last three words. She was surprised when they popped out. Not as surprised as he was. He said, "You do?"

"Yeah, I do. Of course I do."

"I didn't know. I'd stopped believing it."

"You're stupid then. I've been stupid, too. I'm sorry."

"Me too."

"Okay, I know you have to go. Call me when you can. But you be careful. Promise?"

18

Shortly before nine p.m., standing under the *porte cochere* of the Flagler House hotel, Carmine was saying, "I don't care. I'm not riding in one of those things."

Peppers said, "Come on, loosen up a little. Besides, we'll be late otherwise. There's no taxis right now. Bert said don't even think about tryin' to park down there. We gotta grab a Pedi-Cab."

He gestured toward one of the odd little vehicles that was queued up just a few feet away at the curb.

Carmine said, "Not doin' it."

"Why not?"

"It's pink. And it's got this little fringe or some shit all around it. And I don't wanna sit behind some gay guy's ass pumping up and down."

"You don't have to look."

"How do I not look? Guy'd practically be sitting on my face."

Peppers glanced at his watch. "Listen, we're representin' Lou. This guy Bert's doin' us a favor. It's not right we'd be late."

He raised a hand to hail the Pedi-Cab. Carmine had no choice but to go along. The driver's name was Danny. He wore a purple leotard and had legs like a ballet dancer. His buttocks were dimpled where the muscles gave place to the hollows of the hip and it was pretty clear he was wearing a thong. Peppers told him their destination and he said in a friendly voice, "Ah, I don't often bring visitors over there. You gentlemen must be comedy buffs."

Carmine didn't quite understand the comment but he was unhappy with the whole situation and ready to take offense. "Why? We look funny to you?"

Danny thought that was really pretty clever, and he laughed as he pedaled, his sculpted thighs rising up and dipping down like breaching dolphins. "Nice," he said. "Quick. You mostly like stand-up?"

"Standing up, laying down, in a sling, trapeze. Whatever."

Danny laughed at that, too. It wasn't just that he worked for tips and tried to be agreeable. He was genuinely amused by this guy's impression of a New York tough guy; he had the accent down, the gruffness. "Think you'll get up onstage? I mean, you seem like a natural."

Carmine said, "You fucking crazy?"

"Don't be shy," coaxed Danny. "It's just Key West. I bet you'd get a ton of laughs up there."

"Watch yourself, buddy."

This last didn't sound too friendly, though Danny had to admire the way his passenger stayed in character. He pedaled the rest of the way in silence.

🌴 🌴 🌴

Bert, not having a whole lot else to do, had arrived early and was sitting at the mostly empty bar. Pat had made him an Old-Fashioned, which he ordered mainly so he could feed the alcoholic cherry to the dog. Nursing his drink, he watched the proprietress go about her preparations for the rush that probably would never come. Tonight she seemed a bit distracted, a little sluggish maybe, and he asked if she was okay.

"Hm? Yeah...fine. Just seem to have a lot on my mind all of a sudden."

"Anything ya wanna talk about?"

"Thanks, Bert...But no." She'd hesitated an instant because in fact she would have loved to ask the old man's advice about how seriously a friend of hers should take a death threat from a jealous lover who was in the Mafia. Problem was, she couldn't really ask that without presuming that Bert was Mafia too, and while he'd dropped occasional hints in that direction, he'd never come right out and admitted it. Pat was still trying to think of a tactful way to broach the subject, when the club's door swung open and two strangers walked in.

She quickly sized them up: Out-of-towners who probably thought they were perfectly dressed for an evening out in Florida, except their idea of Florida came from a TV show set in South Beach in the 1980s. They wore shiny shirts, open at the neck and halfway down the chest; chains, of course; snug pants that bound them in the crotch. One of them looked like an old-school muscle-man, not really cut like a modern gym-rat but with lots of beef. The other was thin and sort of concave, like you could draw a pretty smooth crescent from the top of his forehead all the way to the tips of his pointy shoes. The newcomers looked around until their eyes met Bert's. The old man shifted his dog, then, trying to hide the effort it cost him, got up slowly from his barstool to greet them.

Pat stood a discreet distance away while the men shook hands. They mostly talked out of the sides of their mouths and she became a notch more certain that Bert was in the Mob.

The newcomers ordered shots and beers. When she delivered them, the beefy guy gave her something like a wink, then jerked a huge thumb toward the bare and as yet unlit stage and said, "So, hon, where's the pole?"

"Pole?"

"I mean, ya know, a set, some props, stuff like that."

"Not our style," Pat said. "Here, what you see is what you get. Our performers are pretty much naked up there."

"Best news I had all day," said the beefy guy.

The concave one said, "Maybe it's better we move to a table."

🌴 🌴 🌴

"Her too?" said Lenny. "You're making her wear a disguise too?"

"Can't be too careful," Ricky said.

"Besides," said Carla, "it's kind of fun. Incognito. Sexy word, right? Besides, when did I ever get to go anywhere in costume? Halloween when I was a little kid. Cheap store-bought skeleton or polyester princess with a cardboard magic wand. This is, like, professional."

Lenny couldn't disagree with that. The disguise was so good that he'd walked right past Carla when he'd first stepped into the Harbor House's lobby to pick them up. Her usually unruly raven hair had been carefully tucked under a reddish wig teased into the kind of lacy but immobile pouf that was standard issue from suburban beauty parlors everywhere. The drama of her wide-set eyes was muted by a dorky pair of glasses with upswept plastic frames, and an inflatable ring around her midriff made her look thirty pounds heavier than she really was. A shapeless dress in a floral pattern completed the outfit and paired perfectly with Ricky's elastic-waist pants, loud plaid sports jacket, narrow moustache, and oily-looking toupee. Together, they looked like a completely forgettable couple playing hooky from a cruise ship or people you might have dinner with, but only once, if you met them on a package bus tour.

With Lenny leading the way, they stepped out into the balmy and electric Key West evening. The air smelled like oyster shells and people out on dates. From the bars of Duval Street, just a block away, came roughly blended sounds of amped music and a swell of rather manic laughter. Scooter horns beeped here and there, red and green flashes from the harbor buoys skimmed across the water. Carla said, "It's so nice out, so alive. Can we walk?"

"Kind of far," said Lenny. "Getting kind of late. I think we ought to grab a cab."

Rather than complain, Carla looked for a compromise. "Open-air, at least? Maybe one of those rickshaw kind of things?"

After strolling half a block they came across a pedi-cab. Its driver had gorgeous legs squeezed into a purple leotard. Lenny gave him the destination and he said, "Wow, you guys are the second fare I've brought over there in the last fifteen, twenty minutes. Last guys were pretty funny, I thought maybe they were warming up an act. Had this kind of deadpan wiseguy shtick going on."

"Sounds like a regular riot," Ricky said.

"Two trips there in an hour," mused the driver as he pedaled off toward Garrison Bight. "Maybe that place is finally catching on."

19

The first performer of the evening was a lesbian comedian with ear grommets and blue hair and whose routine was largely built around the elaborate and ever-escalating excuses she'd had to make to her super-straight and clueless parents back in Iowa for why she wasn't going to the junior prom, the senior prom, the homecoming prom, or the Debutante Ball at the local Grange. She'd claimed tonsillitis, appendicitis, tendinitis, meningitis, vaginitis, diverticulitis, a touch of plague, a hint of bird flu, and needing to stay home and study for a big Home Ec exam for which she had to memorize fifteen different pork chop recipes.

She was five minutes into her set before Carmine finally understood that she wasn't going to take her clothes off. He got even by not laughing at her jokes.

Between acts, the three men chatted. Carmine thought Peppers was trying a little too hard to ingratiate himself with Bert, saying how cute his dog was and how Bert was still a living legend in New York. Even Carmine could see that the old man was bored by the compliments and wanted to talk about other things. He kept trying to work the conversation around to details of Fat Lou's business that they were not supposed to talk about.

"So," he said, "sounds like Lou's got himself a partner down here, well-connected local guy."

"Yup," said Carmine, and pressed his teeth together.

"Neglected to mention his name, though."

"Due respect," said Peppers, "I don't think it was neglect. The name, he wants to keep it under wraps for now."

"Even from me?" the old man said, his curiosity beginning to gnaw like heartburn.

Peppers just offered a deferential shrug.

"Well, okay, I get it. Delicate business, dealing with a local partner. So much based on trust. Then again, the local partner has a built-in edge, namely local knowledge. Which can become a problem if this partner is not the type to play completely fair or divvy up risks and rewards exactly fifty-fifty. If I was Lou, I'd want some local knowledge about the partner wit' the local knowledge. *Capeesh?*"

Peppers said, "Yeah, *capeesh,* but Lou seems to have a pretty good sense a the guy."

Undeterred, Bert said, "And I have a pretty good sense a the Pope, but it ain't the same like I live right there in the Vatican. But okay, whatever. I'm just offerin' ta help. Save you guys some trouble. Spare ya, maybe, from, ya know, screwin' up big time and havin' Lou get all upset with ya even though the screw-up wouldn't really be your fault, it would just be that you lacked for local information that no one could really have expected you to have unless you received it directly from the mouth of a bona fide local who lived here forty years. But okay, if Lou prefers to keep it a secret even from an old friend and ally, I'm sure he has his reasons, and, like I say, if the whole thing turns to shit because of a lack of understanding about who you're dealin' with, then I don't see where you guys could really get the blame. *Salud.*"

He raised what was left of his now-watery cocktail, took a sip, petted his dog, and waited.

He casually watched as Carmine and Peppers consulted with their eyes, and he could read in their wavering expressions the mild but unceasing anguish of underlings just trying to stay out of trouble. Peppers licked his lips. Carmine's mouth twitched at the corner. Bert had the feeling they were just about to spill, but at that moment another comedian stepped onto the stage. Out of politeness, Bert joined in the modest applause and shifted his attention. He thought he'd made a pretty good start at wearing these guys down.

This next comedian was a scrawny guy whose Adam's apple protruded like a knuckle and who looked completely stoned. He futzed around with the microphone for a few seconds then started talking about a dream he'd had a few nights before, in which he was playing ping-pong with Donald Trump.

He was still working on the set-up of the story when the club's door opened and three new, entirely unremarkable people stepped in: A very average-looking guy with a pronounced forward lean to his posture, and a dowdy couple who looked like they'd purchased their resort-wear from a struggling outlet center in the Upper Midwest. Not wanting to disrupt the performance, they stepped very quietly to one side of the room and sat down at a vacant table.

20

The comedian was saying, *"So Trump pulls out this enormous gold paddle and says, 'This one's mine. You, you loser, you have to play with a shoe.'"*

The newcomers settled in, shifted their chairs as silently as they could, tried to pick up the thread of the story.

"So Trump serves the ball. It goes into the net. I say, 'My point.' He says, 'No it isn't.' I say, 'Yeah it is. You served into the net.' He says, 'No. You served into the net!' I say, 'Look where the ball is. It's on your side of the table.' He says, 'No it isn't. It's on your side. One-nothing mine.'"

The comedian paused for effect. During the brief silence, the new arrivals glanced around the room, appraising the very modest turnout. Suddenly Carla dug her long red fingernails into Ricky's forearm. He felt their bite even through the fabric of the plaid sports jacket and shot her a look. She tried hard to keep her whisper from sounding frantic. "Don't move. Don't turn. But, Jesus Christ, it's him! He's here!"

"Next point, we hit a couple back and forth, him with the giant gold paddle, me with the shoe..."

"Who?" said Ricky. "Who's here?"

With her eyes alone, Carla pointed to Carmine, who mostly had his back to them but with enough of his bulk and broke-nosed profile showing that there could be no doubt. Her companions tracked the look.

Ricky hissed, "Shit! Are you fucking kidding me?"

"Then Trump winds up, gets his fat stomach right up against the table, kind of hanging over the table, really, a little bit disgusting, and tries this ginormous smash..."

Rocking forward in his chair, Ricky said, "We gotta get out of here. Right now."

Lenny, to his own surprise, felt relatively calm and clear. "No. No sudden movements. Nothing that would draw attention."

"...that misses the table, misses everything, not even close. Being a nice guy, I say, 'Nice try.' He says, 'Nice try, my ass. That was a great shot I hit. Two for me.'"

Ricky's voice got glassy. "I can't just stay here. My skin's crawling. I'm gonna panic."

Carla stroked his hand. She kept one eye on Carmine's broad and hulking back. He was sitting stone-faced, not laughing.

Lenny whispered, "You're fine, Ricky. Disguise is great. Trust it. What we're gonna do for now, we're gonna sit a while like everything is hunky-dory. No freak-outs, no flying bolts."

"Easy for you to say. You're not the vendetta guy."

"So then Trump says, 'Okay, loser, you try serving one.' So I serve one, with the shoe. It's got some spin on it and it goes right by him. He says, 'Do over. I wasn't ready.' I say, "Weren't ready? You just told me to serve. Now you weren't ready?' He says, 'Wasn't ready. Doesn't count.'"

"We're gonna sit," Lenny resumed, "till there's a natural time to leave, then we're gonna slip out quietly, no rush, no hurry, nothing to make heads turn."

So they sat. Ricky took shallow breaths and tried to will away the cold and itchy sweat that he felt forming at his hairline, under the toupee. The routine about the ping-pong game continued. Trump claimed every point even if he missed the table, threw his paddle, got pissed off and stomped the ball flat, even if his pants fell down in the middle of a rally. The performer's tempo got crisper as the story's momentum built, as its imagery grew more grotesque but also more magically present before the audience's eyes, and the laughs started coming easier, thicker, carrying over from line to line.

Even at the Mafia table, there were some chuckles. Bert gave forth a spasmodic giggle that woke up his dog. Peppers was overtaken by a percussive snort that made him have to blow his nose. Carmine momentarily forgot his stance of stubborn grumpiness and felt a chortle laboring to rise from deep down in his chest, but just then he heard, buried somewhere in the general chorus of laughter, a laugh that was different from all the others and reminded him of one he used to know. It was a laugh like a bell, like the sound of the little triangle that people play in marching bands and whose small bright sound somehow slices through the noise of all the bigger, louder instruments. Carmine knew he wasn't really hearing it. It wasn't possible. It was his imagination, his disappointment mocking him. The laugh lingered in his ears and for a moment he wondered if he was going nuts. His own half-formed laugh died with a metallic taste at the back of his throat.

A few minutes later, when the comedian had finished his act and walked off the bare stage, Carmine finally gave in to the humiliating impulse to swivel around and look in the direction from which the imagined and painful and impossible laugh had come. There was no one sitting there at all.

21

Outside, Ricky had bounded down the gangplank, raced up the dock ramp, and sprinted a block and a half along Roosevelt Boulevard before Carla and Lenny could catch up with him. They found him half bent over with his hands on his knees as he labored to regain his breath. His face was damp and shiny with exertion; his toupee was askew and his thin moustache had come unstuck at one corner. For a moment he said nothing, just wheezed, then he straightened up, wheeled toward Lenny, and with a fury that now stood in for fear, he said, "I got just one question for you. Why the fuck did you set me up?"

Lenny said, "What?"

"You heard me. You set me up, didn't you? Told him I was in Key West. Led me right into the trap."

"Are you crazy, Ricky? Are you demented? Why the hell would I do that?"

"You're mad at me. You're mad I didn't stick around to do your stupid show."

"I'm not mad," Lenny lied. "No, okay, let's be honest, of course I'm mad you didn't stick around to do my stupid show. That stupid show was my future. But I'm not mad to the point of wanting to get you killed. That's just ridiculous."

Ricky looked down at the hard and cheap black shoe that was part of his disguise. His foot was tapping against the sidewalk and he couldn't seem to make it stop. The three of them were standing near a streetlamp at the corner of Eisenhower Boulevard. The streetlamp threw a cone of purplish light in which the plaid pattern of his jacket looked like a schematic drawing of a subway system and the reddish strands of Carla's wig glowed like the coils in a toaster.

"Well, if you didn't set me up," said Ricky, "then why the hell's he here?"

"An excellent question," Lenny said. "I have no idea. But let me ask you one now. I know you're an actor and all, but did it ever occur to you, even for a second, that maybe it isn't about you? That there are other reasons in the universe for why stuff happens?"

Ricky didn't answer that, just looked down at the foot that continued tapping all on its own.

"Or that maybe you should think twice about making crazy accusations against people who are on your side? Or that maybe you just need to pop a couple Xanax, chill the fuck out, and apologize?"

Before he could respond, Carla said, "Too late on the Xanax. I flushed it."

"You *what?*"

"Okay, maybe it was a little optimistic, a little premature. Sorry. I thought things were calming down."

🌴 🌴 🌴

Inside Titters, it was break time. The makeshift stage went briefly dark, people shuffled off to the restrooms or the bar, and Bert the Shirt, in his endlessly patient and quietly relentless way, resumed his nosey quest for information.

"So anyways," he was saying, "if this is just a courtesy call or sentimental journey that Fat Lou asked you to pay on an old and trusted friend, then I'm honored by the gesture and glad to have your company, but if there's more of a tactical or let's say strategic item on youse's agenda, like for instance my helping in some liaison capacity between your usual stompin' ground and the very different turf on which you currently find yourselves, then it would be helpful that I have a little more insight into what it is youse are hoping to accomplish and how I can help prevent the embarrassing spectacle of you falling on your asses while you're tryin' to do it, which, let's face it, is something that can happen all too easily and sometimes wit' disastrous or even fatal consequences when people try t'operate in a neighborhood not their own."

Carmine and Peppers found themselves holding their breath until the old man had finally reached the end of his sentence, a sentence that was more like an aria. Then they shared a glance. Neither of them wanted to admit it, but Bert's insinuations about people screwing up when far from home had touched a nerve. They were not well-traveled guys. They'd seldom been north of the Bronx or south of Philadelphia. They were strangers in Key West. And, so far, what was their experience of the place? They'd been sure they were going to a strip club and instead they ended up at a comedy joint full of lesbians and stoners. If they'd misread that situation so badly, how many others would they misread, and at what cost?

Peppers decided it would be safer in the long run to open up at least a little bit, swap some information. Jack-knifing his concave body low across the table, he said softly, "You know a guy named Ted Clifton?"

At the mention of the name, the drowsy chihuahua in Bert's lap raised its head and let out something between a whimper and a growl. Bert said, "Yeah, I know him."

The goombahs waited for more. Nothing came. Carmine said, "And?"

"And what? I know him."

Peppers said, "Two minutes ago you were givin' way longer answers wit'out there was even a question."

Bert shrugged and petted the dog.

"Ya trust the guy?" Carmine pressed.

"About what?"

"Ya know," said Peppers. "Just in general."

"Just in general? Like, to hold my wallet? Walk my dog? Save me a seat at the movies? All depends what you're askin' do I trust 'im about."

"Let's just call it business," Carmine said, and crossed his arms against his massive chest as if to prevent any further information from leaking out.

"Business," Bert murmured. "In business, no, I wouldn't trust him."

"Why not?" asked Peppers.

"Well, for starters, he already has the bubbas in his pocket, the politicians and the cops and so forth, and he doesn't seem to be hurting in the cash flow department, so what kind of business would it have to be for him to need a partner such as Fat Lou unless it was a business that was not strictly kosher and maybe he just didn't have the balls to do it on his own? What kinda business might that be? That's the question."

"No it ain't," said Peppers, revealing just the first faint hint of irritation. "The question is why wouldn't ya trust 'im?"

"Oh yeah, that. Because he ain't trustworthy."

"That's just sayin' the same thing different," Carmine observed.

"Very astute," said Bert. "Look, bottom line, he's not an honorable guy. Never gets his own hands dirty. But he'll cheat, he'll connive, he'll try to grab more than his share, and, down here at least, he has the lawyers and connections to get away with it. Home field advantage. That's where maybe I can help. But how can I help if I don't even know what we're talkin' about?"

Carmine and Peppers consulted with their eyes and seemed finally to realize they were teaching way more than they were learning. They clammed up and drank their drinks.

A few moments later, the house lights dimmed and the stage lights came on. Thin applause greeted the next performer. Bert stroked his dog and told himself to be content with what he'd teased out of his guests so far. Ted Clifton—slick, tidy, presentable Ted Clifton, with his silk pants and cotton sweaters with the famous logos—was getting into bed with the Mob. That was kind of interesting, and not a bad bit of nosing for just an hour or two of friendly chitchat.

22

At two a.m. Lenny was still wired, shaken up, and baffled by what he'd seen and heard earlier that evening, and he was pacing in Pat's living room when she finally got home from the club. She put away the night's meager receipts, kicked off her shoes, then the first thing she said was, "So, was the material really that bad?"

"Hm?"

"The Trump bit. With the ping-pong. I thought it was really pretty clever."

"Who said it wasn't?"

"You guys walked out," she said. "I saw you slip away the second he finished. Didn't even clap."

"No offense to the comic. I thought the routine was more than decent. A little topical for my taste, but you know me, I go more for the timeless, the universal. But leave that on the side for now. That's not why we bolted. We bolted because the guy who wants to kill Ricky was right there in the room."

"Excuse me?"

"Sitting at a three-top with another Miami Vice-looking guy and a very old man in a red vest with a dog."

"With Bert?"

"I have no idea who he was with. I only know the three of them were sitting at a table maybe fifteen feet away. Carla recognized the old boyfriend even though he mostly had his back to us. We snuck out under cover of a little laughing, and then Ricky accused me of setting him up."

"Setting him up?"

"Yeah, like somehow I ratted him out and arranged the whole thing to get him whacked because I'm mad he didn't do our show."

Pat took a moment to process that, then said, "I need a drink."

"Count me in," said Lenny.

She poured them each some bourbon, neat, and they went out to the backyard. Key West is never completely quiet, but at two a.m. on a weeknight, a good distance from Duval Street, it comes pretty close. The hum of traffic dies away, the honking of scooter horns becomes only a rare annoyance, and mostly what you hear is the rasping of crickets, the soft rustling of palm fronds on every scrap of breeze, and the plaintive voices of invisible tree toads, which bleat like tiny sheep. Lenny took in the lulling symphony, put his feet up on a wicker ottoman, sipped his whisky, and said, "Pretty relaxing here."

"Used to be," said Pat.

"Till I showed up."

"You're the least of it."

"Oh, thanks."

"I mean compared to Ricky being on the lam and the guy who wants to kill him showing up at my club as the guest of one of my very few regulars, who I happen to think of as a friend."

"The old man? He's a friend?"

She nipped at her bourbon. "Maybe that's a stretch. But he comes in two, three times a week, usually early when there's hardly anyone around. We chat. He's a nice guy, probably lonely. Has some pretty good stories from New York. I always sort of wondered if he was Mafia or just from Brooklyn. I guess now we know."

Lenny said nothing for a moment, just gazed contemplatively at the peaceful blue light that shimmered through and above the water of the swimming pool. Then he said, "Wonder what's in it for him."

"What's in what for who?"

"For the old man. Getting Ricky killed."

Pat put her drink down harder than she meant to and it made a sharp sound against the little glass table. "Now wait a second—"

Leaning forward at the waist and neck, Lenny didn't wait. "I mean, what's his angle on it? *Cosa nostra* loyalty oath? Some code of honor bullshit?"

"Hold on. Please. They happened to be there together. We can't just assume that Bert's involved."

"We can't? Why can't we? How else does this Carmine guy end up at your club? Coincidence?"

"Coincidences happen," Pat said.

"In clusters? Like, the guy who wants to ice Ricky, who happens to be Mafia and from New York, just happens to walk into your club half a continent away? And he just happens to be shepherded by another guy who also happens to be Mafia? That's a lot of coincidences."

Pat was shaking her head. "I just can't imagine Bert would be part of something like that. He's practically a hundred. He has a little dog."

"Maybe Hitler had a little dog. A dachshund probably. Maybe a schnauzer. So what?"

"Maybe," Pat countered, "they're just old friends from the City. Maybe it has nothing to do with Ricky. Does Bert even know who Ricky is? How would he know he was in town?"

"You said the old man's a regular, right? Did he happen to be there the other night when Ricky came in naked?"

"Well, yeah, he was," admitted Pat. "But he wouldn't have recognized him."

"Why not? You did."

"That was because of the routine, the *Star-Spangled Banner* bit. I wouldn't've recognized him just by his looks. I don't think anybody would've. No way."

Lenny sipped his bourbon and looked up at the stars. They dimmed and brightened as otherwise invisible wisps of cloud scudded by beneath them. Finally he said, "Look, Pat, I'm a gag writer, not a freakin' Sherlock, but it seems to me there are two possibilities for how Carmine gets to your club. Either it's a long-ass series of coincidences, or else Bert brings him there to get him close to Ricky. I know you hate that idea, but doesn't it seem logical?"

"Logical, okay. But I just don't buy it in my gut. There's gotta be another explanation."

"Let's hear it then. I'm all ears."

She pressed her lips together so firmly that they almost folded up between her teeth. She always did this when she was concentrating really hard, and, way back when she and Lenny used to flirt, he'd found it adorable. Now she held the clench until her mouth went white at the corners, then finally said, "What if Carmine's being in Key West has nothing at all to do with Ricky? Nothing whatsoever?"

"Okay, let's roll with that. Then why's he here?"

"Who knows? Why's anyone in Key West? Vacation? Midlife crisis? Maybe he's here on business. Different business, I mean."

Lenny volleyed that right back. "*Different* business? Pat, it's a small island. How many Mafia gigs are available on a given day? He's going to have another one aside from whacking Ricky? Double-dipping in this little outpost? Possible, I guess, but doesn't it sound like piling on just one more coincidence?"

She started raising a hand to protest, then let it slowly fall and curl around her whisky glass instead. Looking off at the blanket of blue light above the pool, she said wearily, "Yeah, I guess it does. Can't even convince myself there's a better explanation." She lifted the glass to her lips but put it down again without drinking. "Just makes me feel a little sick to think that Bert is helping out a killer."

23

Next morning, not early, Bert gently put his dog down on the drain board next to the kitchen sink, then untangled the coiled wire of his landline phone and called Fat Lou. Dispensing with pleasantries, he said, "I met your geniuses last night and I'm reporting back. Here's my report: I was not impressed."

At home in Bay Ridge, the New York boss was having breakfast. His wife had made him a hubcap-sized frittata with hunks of sweet sausage in it. The sausage contained fennel seeds that now and then got stuck in his teeth. While continuing to eat and at the same time talking on the phone, he also managed to unseat the wedged particles with a fingernail and to arrange them in a circle on the paper napkin next to him. Chewing, he said to Bert, "Didn't think you'd be."

"Those two numb-nutses goin' head-to-head with Ted Clifton? Trust me, it's not a good idea."

Sounding annoyed but not surprised, Lou said, "They told you who the partner was? They wasn't supposed to say that wit'out I gave permission."

"Well, they did. They leaked like sieves. They folded like a cheap umbrella." He gave the dog a wink. The dog looked at him with awe.

Lou grunted or maybe burped. "They spill what the business is, too?"

"Nah, I didn't get that out of 'em," Bert admitted. "Ten minutes more, I woulda. But I ran outa time. Another comedian came on."

"Comedian?"

"Yeah, I took 'em to a comedy club. Which is another strange thing about these knuckleheads. When I tol' 'em where we were meeting, they sounded all excited, then, when we was sittin' there, they hardly cracked a smile. Strange birds."

Fat Lou folded another slab of frittata into his face and talked around it. "So what's the problem with havin' 'em sit down with Clifton?"

"The problem is that, in this particular case or let's say instance, two heads ain't better than one, 'cause two heads ain't very bright. Whereas Clifton is. Now, your business, whatever it happens to be, I'm gonna assume that by its very essence or let's say the nature of the beast, it entails some kind of risk and that, should things not go well or even reach a point of being all fucked up, someone's gonna take the fall. Who's that gonna be? Clifton? No, he doesn't work that way. Lemme tell ya a story."

In Bay Ridge, Fat Lou rolled his eyes and gestured to his wife to pour more coffee into his gargantuan mug.

"Couple years ago," Bert went on, "this big housing project went belly up. Investors got wiped out. Developer went to jail for fraud. Except, guess what? The schmuck who went to jail, that wasn't the real developer, he was the guy that Clifton put in the hot seat. Couple years before that, there was this big road improvement contract except the roads didn't get improved. Clifton's front guy is still in the Pen. Year before that—"

"Okay, okay, I get the picture," Fat Lou interrupted. "But what I can't quite figure is why you give a shit about my guys maybe falling on their faces."

"Why?" said Bert, and he took a moment to think the question through. "Well, call me sentimental, but I still have certain loyalties. Up to a point, at least. And aside from that, it's like this. In my book, there's bad guys and there's worse guys. Bad guys at least admit they're crooks, outlaws, whatever. Worse guys pretend they aren't. I got no respect for that. Frosts me to see shitheads like that keep comin' out on top."

"You forget he's my partner on this."

"You picked him. I didn't."

Fat Lou brought forth a leisurely and thoughtful belch. "So now you're sayin' I gotta worry about him screwin' me?"

"I'm just sayin' that if there's an edge to be grabbed, he'll grab it, and your knuckleheads got no chance."

Lou's wife silently removed the empty frittata plate and presented her husband with a prune Danish the size of a laptop. He poked his finger into the prune part and licked it. Then he said, "Okay, how much you want?"

"Want for what?"

"Ya know, for kind of overseein' the negotiations."

"I don't recall ever sayin' I was interested in doin' that."

"Fifty? A hundred? Come on, Bert, name your price."

The old man hesitated, staring rather blankly at the chihuahua in the drain board. Too late, as happened to him from time to time, he realized he'd been talking his way into a deeper involvement than he'd intended at the start or even thought he wanted; except apparently he did. Finally he said, "Lou, there is no price. I don't take money. You know that."

"And I don't take up a guy's valuable time and expertise wit'out I pay for it. Call it one twenty-five if things work out."

"And what if they don't?"

"Then no one makes bupkis and hopefully we're still friends. Okay, I'll go one-fifty. Final offer."

"But this is nuts. One-fifty for what? I don't even know—"

"You'll come up to speed. You always have before. You'll take a meeting or two, you'll find out everything you need to know."

Bert frowned and looked at his dog. The little creature shot him back a knowing and somewhat smug glance, as if it had figured from the start where things were headed. Wanting to hold his ground on something at least, the old man said, "The money, Lou. All I'm gonna do is give it away. Humane Society. Kittens. Puppies. Baby birds that fell onna ground."

"What you do with it, I don't give a shit. I only give a shit I pay it. I feel much better having you involved. I'll tell my guys you're in on everything from now on."

24

Over eggs Benedict and a bottle of Prosecco at a rolling table in their room, Carla said, "I don't want to be a nag, but I really think you owe Lenny an apology."

She was braced for a denial and a disagreement, but none came. Instead, Ricky said in a mild, even momentarily humble, monotone, "Yeah, you're right. I owe Lenny an apology. I owe Pat an apology. I owe my agent an apology. I owe everybody an apology. I've been messing things up for everyone."

Disarmed by this spasm of remorse, she reached gently for his wrist and said with partial accuracy, "No one blames you, honey. And one of these days you'll get a chance to make it up to everyone. Especially yourself."

He didn't seem to believe it. He gave his eyebrows a dubious and gloomy lift and sipped some wine.

She said, "You regret it, Ricky?"

"Hm?"

"Picking me up."

At that he finally smiled. "Hey, I didn't pick you up. You picked me up. With the whole cast of *The Sopranos* sitting right there at your table. Pretty ballsy. And no, I don't regret it."

It didn't occur to him to ask her if she felt the same. Why wouldn't she? He stabbed an egg yolk with a spear of toast and asked her how she was enjoying brunch.

"Oh, it's great," she said, but she said it in the underwhelmed tone of a three-star review. "I mean, the sauce is yummy and I love Prosecco but I wouldn't say it exactly feels like brunch. Brunch is, like, ya go out, there's ferns, other people, waiters, you smell bacon, maple syrup when the trays go by. It's, ya know, a going out thing, a being around people thing. You think we could open up the doors to the balcony, at least?"

He said nothing, just glanced uneasily at the closed and double-locked doors with the translucent curtain still drawn across them. Beyond the balcony there was nothing but the pool area and the twinkling green water of the harbor, seamed and cross-stitched with the wakes of yachts and skiffs, made somehow jovial by the roly-poly movement of red and green buoys on the surging current. The tableau could hardly have been more peaceful, but no scene is peaceful to a man who feels hunted.

Nevertheless, trying to be accommodating, Ricky stood up, sidled with cat-like movements toward the dreaded window and twitched back the curtain. He undid the locks with slightly trembling fingers, and threw open the doors while simultaneously diving away from the flood of sunlight that poured in. He edged around the room's dim perimeter to return to his seat at the rolling table and was in a sweat by the time he got there.

Mopping his forehead with his napkin, he said, "I think my pulse just went up to a hundred forty. Look, this is pathetic. I admit it. I'm a wreck and I need to get out of this town. Travel awhile. Go someplace else."

"And what would that accomplish?" Carla said. "Just more running. You can't hide out forever, Ricky."

"No, but I don't have to sit here like a quailing zombie either."

She tapped her long red fingernails against her wine glass. They made a muted bell sound that was almost like her laugh. "Well, you know what I think? I really think the safest place you could be for now is right where you are."

"Here? Trapped with him on this dinky little island?"

"The whole world's a dinky little island if you're running scared. But think about it; here we have a big advantage. We know he's here. He doesn't know we're here."

"What makes you so sure of that?"

"For one thing," she said, "we had pretty good disguises. And he never even looked around at us. Not once. Believe me, if he had any inkling we were there, he would have come after us, like, pronto. I know the man. That's how he is. Doesn't plan. No restraint. He just goes. So if he didn't go for you, that means he had no idea."

Ricky chewed a knuckle and thought that over. "But if he doesn't know we're here, why the hell's *he* here?"

With as much certainty as she could muster, she said, "Well, it wouldn't be for fun, that much I'm pretty sure of. He hates Florida. I used to ask him to take me to Miami. He'd say it was too far. I said I'd settle for Orlando. He'd just shake his head and say *Florida don't show me nothin'*. Besides, if he was here for fun he'd have a girlfriend hanging on his arm, and there wasn't any girlfriend. So it must just be a job."

"Oh, just a job," said Ricky as he reached into the ice bucket and poured out the last of the Prosecco. "Just a little head-bashing or throat-slitting or stuffing somebody into the trunk. Just another day at the office, la-di-da."

"Actually," said Carla, "his being on a job, that's like the best news we could get. He'll have other things on his mind. So he does the job, he leaves town, maybe he calms down by then, maybe we have a better read on him by then. In the meantime you and I can chill a little. Maybe even see Key West. Kind of a shame to be here and not really see it."

"Kind of a shame to see it from a car trunk," said Ricky.

"It'll be okay," said Carla. "Trust me, the guy has no idea we're here. How's the supply of disguises holding up?"

25

Lenny should not have been surprised that his call to Marsha got forwarded to voicemail. That's what happened to most calls, after all. Even so, he was disappointed to be hearing the robo-voice instead of his wife's, and the tedious interval in which the caller's options were recited for the millionth time somehow threw him off his rhythm. The message he left sounded, even in his own ears as he was leaving it, rushed and rambling and maybe a little bit hysterical.

While the message was landing in her silenced phone, Marsha was teaching a class to a couple dozen bored sophomores. It wasn't their fault they were bored. Their teacher was hung over from her unaccustomed binge the night before and was giving a very uninspired and disjointed lecture about the themes of honor and vengeance in *The Iliad*. Marsha herself was bored by what she was saying and it was all she could do not to yawn back at the yawning faces in front of her.

As she labored through the seemingly endless fifty minutes, her mind began running on two very separate and parallel tracks. On one track, more or less by rote, she continued extolling the glories of great literature by dead geniuses; on the other track, she was thinking about the messy, sloppy, unelevated but precious business of real life. She'd been neglecting that side of things lately; the haze of her hangover, paradoxically, was allowing her to see that very clearly now. She'd been reading life too much and living it too little, letting the politics of the moment and her presumably sturdy academic judgments stand in for raw emotion. Life unfolded day to day...and she regarded it and criticized...and wondered why these two strands, the actual and the perfect, didn't quite connect.

The parallel strands of her thinking didn't stay parallel for long, however. Inevitably, they began to muddle up together, and she found herself vaguely blaming *The Iliad* for the troubles she and Lenny had been having. She'd accused her husband of not being serious. Why? Because he didn't strut around like an epic hero, sure of his cause, righting wrongs with grim determination, out to change the world? Face it, that just wasn't Lenny. He wasn't hero material. Funny people hardly ever were because irony killed certainty; and without certainty, heroism was just showing off. No, Lenny and Lenny's destiny were actual-size, ordinary, modest. No shame there; so was almost everybody's. So was hers. How many women got to launch a thousand ships, after all? So why couldn't she put aside the bloated ideals of grad school and just accept the small, sweet, unheroic satisfactions of a married life that didn't change the world and didn't count for much to anyone except the people living it?

Distracted, detached, feeling increasingly blue and at odds with herself, she soldiered through to the end of the lecture then walked to her favorite coffee shop at the edge of campus. She ordered a *macchiato* and was waiting for it to be delivered when she checked her phone and saw that she had a message from her husband. The coffee shop was noisy with the hiss of steaming milk and the clank of trays on tables, so she had to squeeze the phone hard against her ear to hear; the intimate pressure of cold glass against her face lent a frosty urgency to the message and made her husband's voice sound especially breathy and pinched.

"Marsha? It's me. So glad we talked last night. Maybe we're okay now. I hope so...But listen, I have no idea when I might be coming home. It's not about us. Not anymore...But what's going on down here, it's gotten pretty scary. The guy who wants to kill Ricky, he's in Key West. I was sitting maybe twenty feet away from him last night. Watching comedy. Trying to laugh. Kind of terrifying. Don't know how this plays out, just know I have to see it through. No choice, really. I have to. Okay, gotta go. Take care. Love you. Bye."

Sitting there alone in the bustling coffee shop, she listened to the message three times, four, and grew more agitated with each hearing.

Was this really her Lenny? Just ten minutes before, she'd been reconciling herself to the fact that he was not cut out to be a hero, and now all of a sudden he was sounding like he *was* one. But with no experience, no training, no natural leaning toward that sort of thing. What the hell was he thinking?

He was in danger, that much was clear. Sitting twenty feet from a killer. Determined to stay. Doing this to protect someone who wasn't even a friend, not really, just a guy in trouble. Why? Could it be because she'd thrown it in his face that he should be more serious? Was that why he was doing these reckless and possibly fatal things now? To prove himself worthy in her eyes and his own? Would it be her fault if God forbid...

The questions tweaked her, but the more she thought about them, the more she realized they really didn't matter. All that mattered was that her husband was in danger, and far away. And that, in turn, made a lot of things seem simpler and clearer than they had for a very long time. Quite suddenly, without even exactly making a decision, she knew what she had to do. She had to be near him, share the peril, help deal with this bit of down-and-dirty seriousness that real life had thrown in their way. Sitting there in the coffee shop, she got busy on the phone and started making arrangements for a trip to Florida.

26

"Bert," said Ted Clifton, rising from an impressive chrome-and-leather chair behind his desk, "this is an unexpected pleasure." He said it with a pinched smile that enhanced rather than muted the sarcasm.

"Likewise," the old man said, flashing the smile right back at him while at the same time flexing his chihuahua's paw in a sardonic little wave. "Hello from Nacho, too." The dog bared its teeth and whimpered.

"But I don't quite understand," the businessman went on, "what you're doing at this meeting." He didn't look at Bert as he said this, but rather at the two young mobsters who flanked him, looking tough but somewhat sheepish.

Neither Peppers nor Carmine answered, so Bert did it for them. "So happens the gentleman who employs these fine fellas—Fat Lou, or probably Luigi or maybe even Louis Benedetti as you would know him—asked me to advise or counsel or maybe you could even say mentor these relative newbies in the business so that if they happened to find themselves out of their depth or let's say at a disadvantage *vis-à-vis* someone who was the type a person to take advantage of someone at a disadvantage...Hang on a sec, where was I goin' wit' this?...Right. So because I think a deal should be a fair deal and if someone's gonna get fucked he should at least be well-informed enough so that he can pick the appropriate moment to bend over, I agreed to serve as kind of an interpreter of our local customs and to make sure that Peppers and

Carmine here didn't, either from an excess of enthusiasm or lack of perspicacity, do something they would later regret, possibly in prison. In other words, to put it simple, I'm here to help."

With a sourness he couldn't quite mask, Clifton said, "That isn't what Mr. Benedetti and I agreed. We agreed that he was sending down two men."

"And he did," said Bert. "Me, he didn't have to send. I was already here."

Flicking his eyes back and forth between Peppers and Carmine, searching as always for some psychological edge, Clifton said, "Doesn't suggest a lot of confidence in you two gentlemen."

"Ain't about confidence," Carmine growled, though he couldn't come up with an alternate explanation.

After an uncomfortable pause, Bert said, "So, are you gonna invite us to sit down or are we going to conduct this sit-down standing up?"

Grudgingly, Clifton motioned his visitors toward chairs. Bert took a moment to look around the office. It was a beautiful office in a beautiful building on the waterfront in Truman Annex. Everything had been so painstakingly refurbished to look like old Key West that it didn't look like Key West at all. The wood floors gleamed, the whitewashed walls showed just a hint of the grain of the timbers underneath the paint. Big windows gave onto an immaculately level brick walkway, beyond which was a snug marina full of polished sailboats of which no parts seemed to be broken. Real Key West boats never looked like that.

"All right," Ted Clifton said, "I assume you've been filled in on the nature of our business."

"Only briefly," said Bert. "As I understand it from our young friends here, you hope to launch a ferry service to Havana, and in order to do that you have to build a terminal, and in order to build a terminal you have to procure a suitable location, and it's my guess or let's say inference based on the out-of-town partnership you've put together, that procuring said location might very possibly require the maiming or murder or at least scaring the shit out of the current occupant of the premises."

The businessman made a steeple of his fingertips and flexed them lightly. "I've never said anything like that. Let's be clear. What I've said is that I wish to lawfully obtain a lease on such a property and that I hope to lawfully persuade the current lease-holder that it is in her interests to sell the lease to me."

"Okay, let's be clear," Bert echoed, swiveling in turn toward each of the two men sitting alongside him. "Ya see, this is where having an interpreter comes in handy. When he says *lawfully persuade* and this and that other bullshit, what he means is maim, murder or scare the shit out of, except he personally is somewhere else and has an alibi. *Capeesh?*"

He was unhurriedly turning his eyes back toward Clifton, when something unsettling finally hit him. "But wait a sec. Did you just say *her* interests?"

Innocently, the businessman said, "Yes, I did. The current lease-holder is a woman. Your friends here didn't tell you that?"

"No, they didn't."

"Hey, no one told us neither," chimed in Peppers, sounding more than a bit miffed about it.

"Kinda changes things," Carmine added.

"No it doesn't," said Clifton. "Business is business. It doesn't a change a thing."

Peppers said, "If it comes to roughin' up somebody—"

"I've never suggested violence," the businessman interrupted.

"If it comes to roughin' up a woman," Carmine put in anyway, "I just don't see where we would do that."

"Look, man, woman, I'm trying to get a deal done. And it so happens that the woman in question is as tough and stubborn as any man I know."

"That don't make her not a woman," Peppers said. "We got our standards, Mr. Clifton."

"Our self-respect," said Carmine, puffing out his chest.

While this discussion of the finer points of chivalry was underway, Bert was pursuing his own thoughts, and the process was causing him anguish. A woman? A tough-minded woman with a lease on a waterfront property where a ferry terminal might go? How many of those could there be in little old Key West? Hoping he might be wrong, he said, "Excuse me, but moving on from this sensitivity training regarding gender issues, perhaps it would be useful or *a propos* to talk about specifically who this woman is."

Clifton leaned back in his gorgeous chair, crossed his arms against his soft pink chest, fixed Bert with his cold blue eyes and said, "I think you know. It's Pat Coates and it's Titters."

"That dump we were at last night?" Carmine blurted. "Christ, one match and a splash'a gas, and that shithole is history."

"Now, now," said the businessman, casting a quick nervous look at Bert, "we don't need to talk about anything like that."

But then, sensing a chance to win allies, to gain momentum, he circled back and continued on. "But it *is* a dump, isn't it? And it's losing money anyway. And it shouldn't take any violence to get it, just some...convincing. But Bert here, while he's posing as this all-wise and totally neutral mediator, happens to be chummy with the owner. Which is an obvious conflict of interest and nothing but a headache. Which is why, Bert, I really think it's better if you just forget you were even at this meeting and stay the hell out of the way."

Bert petted his dog. He stole glances at Peppers and Carmine, who'd somewhat resented his presence from the start and who now, in response to this conflict of interest gambit, seemed to be leaning toward siding with Clifton. Doing the math, that made three men who wished he would just shut up and go home, and for the space of a long-held breath he wondered if he should do exactly that.

What's the worst that would happen if he just quit and dropped out of the picture? He doubted they'd kill Pat Coates. He hoped they wouldn't hurt her badly. They'd need to intimidate her, of course, find ways to make it impossible for her to run her business. Torching the joint would be one time-honored way of doing that, though there were plenty of others. If she continued to be stubborn, she'd probably end up with nothing; if she wised up and played ball, maybe she could walk away with a few bucks in her pocket. And Titters would be gone, her dream of running a club would be over along with the laughs, and another victory would be chalked up for the bad guys in league with the worse guys.

By instinct more than by thought, Bert decided in that moment that he would not shut up and not go home. He heard himself say, "Hol' on a minute. You guys got me wrong. What makes you think I'm neutral? Did I ever say I was neutral?"

No one answered the question and Bert stayed on the offensive. Leaning forward across the slightly squished chihuahua in his lap, he put a firm hand on Clifton's desk.

"Fat Lou happens to be a very old friend of mine. A sworn friend, if you catch my drift. Pat Coates is a casual acquaintance. Do I like her? Yeah, she's okay. But where's my greater loyalty? Come on, you really think that's a tough call for me?"

Clifton's blue gaze was still chilly and suspicious but maybe a notch less downright hostile than it had been a minute before. Carmine and Peppers shared a glance and squirmed as their sympathies kept wobbling back and forth.

Looking for a clincher, Bert said, "And another thing. You guys think I'm here for my health? You don't think I have a stake in how this thing plays out? You don't think I'm anglin' for a payday, just like youse? You score, I score. Whaddya think I'm livin' on, a fuckin' pension?"

The two goombahs looked sideways at each other. They'd been wondering why this old geezer was taking the time and trouble to school them and shepherd them around. Suddenly they understood. He was doing it for money. Of course he was; it was the way of the world. Why look any farther for his motives?

Confident that he'd won them over at least for the moment, Bert went on, "But about this woman thing, it so happens I agree with Ted. When it comes to business, man, woman, doesn't matter. What matters is we need her out of there. And we'll get her out of there. I think we all agree on that, right?"

He looked from face to face. Peppers and Carmine were nodding solemnly. Ted Clifton allowed himself no expression whatsoever.

"On'y question is how we do it. My preference is that we do it wit'out anyone goes to the hospital, the morgue, or the Pen. Let's call that Plan A. Plan A doesn't work, we up the ante as required. But inna meantime, we do things like I say. Agreed?"

PART THREE

27

Lenny had agreed to help out as bartender that evening. His repertoire of cocktails was pretty limited, but there weren't many customers to serve, and most of them just ordered beers or wine or shots or margaritas. By ten pm, the first few acts had come and gone, leaving a few chuckles in their wake. In the tip jar at a corner of the stage were some dollar bills, a five, and a crumpled twenty that a drunk had dropped in by mistake.

Another comedian took the stage, acknowledged the smattering of applause as though it had been a great ovation, and launched straight into a riff about New York. *"Great place, great place, but ya gotta know how to handle it, ya gotta speak the lingo, ya gotta prove ya belong or they'll eat ya alive. Like the first time I went there. I was very green. A nice, polite kid from the Midwest...Yeah, don't laugh, I was nice and polite back then. But I didn't wanna be taken for a rube and get mugged, ripped off, whatever. So I decided I wasn't gonna say a word until I was sure I could pass for local. Not a single word. Not hello, not goodbye, not nothing. So for a few days I just studied up. I watched, I listened. Finally I had it down, I knew how to sound like a real New Yorker. So I go up to this guy in the subway and say, 'Excuse me, sir, could you please tell me what time it is or should I just go fuck myself?'"*

At that moment the door of the club swung open and Bert and Peppers and Carmine came walking in.

Lenny's mouth went dry at the sight of them. He wondered if they had guns hidden in their pants, knives strapped against their ankles. He drew himself a little beer and quickly drank it down to get his throat to open.

The three men moved silently and slowly toward the bar. The two young ones had shiny shirts on; the shirts were a dark red that reminded Lenny of drying blood that was still sticky and just starting to scab over. The old man wore a monogrammed silk pullover in a funereal midnight blue. Even the dog looked somber.

Trying to sound practiced and blasé, as if Mafia assassins sat down right in front of him all the time, Lenny managed a meek hello and asked what they would like to drink. The young guys asked for shots and beers. Bert asked for an Old-Fashioned. Not wanting to admit he didn't know how to make one, Lenny said, "Um, we're out of those."

"Out of those?"

His poise leaking quickly away, Lenny gave an awkward shrug.

"Just gimme a beer. And a couple cherries with a little bourbon in a saucer for the dog."

With unsteady hands, the fill-in bartender delivered the drinks.

"Pat around?" asked Bert.

"She's in the back."

Peppers let a smirk stretch across his concave face. "This place has a back? The front looks like a back."

Lenny let that pass and went to get her. She was working in what had been the engine room many years ago, when Titters was a houseboat that could actually move. Now the cramped chamber was mainly a holding tank for burned-out spotlights, cables with rotted insulation, chairs and barstools with splintering legs—all the things that needed fixing and most of which would never get fixed. She was wrestling with a length of duct tape when Lenny said, "Your friend Bert's here with the butchers. You still think he isn't trying to lead them to Ricky?"

She said nothing, just wiped her sticky fingers on a rag and headed through the low doorway to the bar, Lenny following a discreet two steps behind. With a brave attempt at a smile, she splayed her hands out on the slab of wood that separated her from her worrisome guests, wished them good evening, and asked if they were having fun.

"We ain't here for fun," said Carmine.

This was exactly the kind of confrontational approach that Bert would have counseled against, and he tried to undo it with some softer words. "What he means to say is we haven't settled in yet, haven't really relaxed."

Unhelpfully, Peppers added, "Ain't heard nothin' funny yet either."

Pat could not help saying, "Maybe you're just not in the mood to laugh. Maybe some other place would suit you better."

"You suggesting we leave?" demanded Carmine.

"Not at all. I just like my guests to be happy."

Bert fed his dog a maraschino cherry and gestured vaguely behind him at the rest of the room. "Guests seem happy. Just too bad there isn't more of 'em."

Pat shrugged.

"Must be tough. The rent. The overhead."

She shrugged again, but by now there was getting to be a tension in her shoulders that would not allow them to drop back into their normal posture.

"That lease must be a burden," the old man went on in the same mild tone. "Month in, month out, season, off-season, money's always due."

Pat said nothing. Her wrists were starting to hurt from the way she was leaning on the bar. A sick metallic taste was rising from the pit of her stomach; her body seemed to be realizing more quickly than her mind that something was going very wrong between herself and this nice old man she'd thought of as a friend.

ONE BIG JOKE

"Course," he went on, "it's bad news, good news. Lotta times, a business isn't doin' so hot, it's the lease where the value is. Lotta times it's worth way more to somebody else."

"Like Ted Clifton?" Pat spat out the words like she'd bitten into something rotten.

"He might be an interested party."

At that, the thugs closed ranks on either side of Bert and curled in with their outside shoulders. Absurdly, they looked in that moment like a vocal trio clustering toward a microphone before breaking into three-part harmony.

Pat didn't want to give ground, but by instinct she fell back half a step. Then she said, "Excuse my slowness, Bert. I'm new at this. Just why are you guys here? You here to scare me? Threaten me? Does it really take three guys?"

"Threaten? No. No one's making threats. Just asking you to consider possibilities. To think about where your interest lies. Ted Clifton is not an unreasonable man. He's willing to pay for things he wants. You could come out okay. Think it over."

With that, he reached into a chest pocket of his silk pullover, just below the fancy monogram, and produced a small and neatly folded piece of paper. He nudged it across the bar toward Pat. "Here's my number," he went on. "Call me anytime if you'd like to discuss your options."

Mustering as much defiance as she could, she pushed the paper back toward him. "Thanks, but there's nothing to discuss."

He left it sitting on the bar as he began the labored process of rising from his stool, the woozy dog cradled in his arm. "Keep it anyway. Just in case. You never know."

🌴 🌴 🌴

When they'd left, Pat poured stiff drinks for herself and Lenny and tossed hers back with a trembling hand. The fear that she hadn't had time to feel while the mobsters were confronting her was now, in retrospect, flooding in like a polluted tide. But even more than fear, she just felt disappointment. Shaking her head, she said, "The old man shilling for Clifton. How's it possible to be so wrong about someone?"

Not wanting to make his old pal feel even worse, Lenny said nothing.

"Go ahead," she went on without rancor. "You can say I told you so. You were right. I was wrong. You saw right away that old Bert was a Judas."

"Except I wasn't right," he admitted. "Not even close. I thought the whole thing was about Ricky and the jealous boyfriend. I had no idea that...that..."

"That they're here to shake me down and take my place away?"

"I didn't want to come right out and say it. But yeah, I guess that's why they're here."

With a quick bitter laugh, Pat said, "Well, I get that much satisfaction, at least. I nailed it that there's some other reason they're in town."

Lenny thought that over for a moment while he sipped his drink. A joke was cracked on stage. A few laughs came from the audience. Then he said, "So if they're really here about the club, where the hell does that leave Ricky?"

28

Except for the Mafia shakedown, it turned out to be a pretty good evening at Titters. There was never exactly a rush, but customers kept drifting in and at some point, as if by stealth, the place had gotten nearly full. The money in the tip jar had risen halfway to the brim, and as the audience approached a kind of critical mass, the performers started seeming funnier. Laughs became contagious, spreading from table to table, bouncing from mind to mind, rippling back and gaining energy like colliding waves.

By midnight, the bar was crowded enough that Lenny and Pat were working side by side. It was only then, while she was mopping up some beer foam with a dishrag, that she noticed the neatly folded piece of paper that Bert had left behind. The sight of it offended and depressed her in the midst of the modestly successful evening and she nearly threw it in the trash. Then, without exactly knowing why, she stuffed it into a pocket of her jeans instead, and promptly forgot about it.

By closing time, the two friends were too worn out even to talk. They did a cursory clean-up, locked the door, and headed home to the perfect little house on Pine Street. After a comradely hug goodnight, Pat went up the porch steps to the front door and Lenny made his way through the tangled and fragrant side-yard to his glorified cabana by the pool.

He was so tired that he didn't even turn a light on when he got inside. He undressed in the dark, left his clothes in a pile on the floor, threw some water on his face, brushed his teeth, had a pee, and got into bed.

Actually, he got halfway into bed.

Then he realized there was a body there. His naked backside, expecting empty air and the cool feel of a sheet, encountered skin and what felt like a knee instead.

Adrenaline scorched his nerves from head to toe and he frantically sprang up again. His feet got tangled in his abandoned clothes and he let out a half-stifled little shriek. His hair was standing on end, his testicles were retreating upward toward his abdomen, and by instinct he began groping in the dark for a weapon, any weapon. His hand found the borrowed tennis racquet and he raised it as high as he could as though to hit a murderous smash. His feet were planted, back arched, abs tensed, shoulder muscles loaded...

That was when the bedside lamp came on. It was not a bright lamp but its suddenness was blinding. From somewhere behind the glare came a familiar voice. "Funny time to practice your overhead, Lenny."

"Marsha?"

"And you forgot to put your shorts on."

"Marsha, what the—?"

"Come to bed. I've missed you."

"But how—?"

"We'll talk tomorrow. Come to bed."

In the bedroom of the main house, Sam was sleeping soundly, as she always did after many hours on the court. Pat went over, smoothed the cotton blanket that lay across her shoulder, and kissed her lightly on the nape of her neck. They saw so little of each other during season. Day shift, night shift, never a whole weekend together. Maybe one of these years they'd get their schedules aligned. She supposed that would be one good thing, at least, about having the club taken away from her. But damn it, she didn't want to let the club be taken away and she didn't plan to let it happen.

She got undressed. While hanging up her jeans, she noticed the slight bulge that Bert's folded paper made in one of the pockets. Shaking her head in remembered disappointment, she plucked it out and, for the second time, was just on the brink of throwing it away when she decided, out of simple curiosity, to look at it.

She wasn't expecting much. She wasn't really expecting anything except a phone number she had no intention of ever calling. To her surprise, the note contained some words as well. They'd been written with a smudgy pencil in a small, crabbed script and they weren't easy to make out. She sat down on the edge of the bed, switched on her reading light, and squinted. Finally she could read the message. *Don't believe everything you hear. Bert.*

That's all it said. She read it over and over again, trying to make it say more, but it refused. She knew what she wished it said, but she didn't want to go too far believing that because what if it was just another ploy, another lurking disillusionment? If she shouldn't believe everything she heard, why should she believe everything she read? On the other hand, if everything was as it had seemed earlier that evening, why would he have bothered writing at all? Then again, why would the old man be double-agenting his own allies, and how likely was it that he'd be passing seditious notes right under their noses? Then again...then again...then again.

She folded up the paper and placed it on her night table. She switched off the lights and snuggled into bed knowing that, wiped out though she was, she probably wouldn't sleep. She tried lying on her left side, her right side, her back, her tummy, but no matter how she turned, the simple words of Bert's message kept turning with her, teasing and tweaking her deep into the shortening night.

29

"What if it's a trap?" said Lenny, at the breakfast table set for four late next morning.

In front of him was a gorgeous poolside spread of melons and juices and cereal and muffins, all put together by Sam and Marsha, who'd been awake for hours. Envious flies hovered near the goodies and people brushed them casually away. The pool pump softly hummed. The air was fresh and smelled not of flowers but of the green and milky buds that flowers sprang from.

Pat, badly rested and still on her first cup of coffee, said, "Look, all I'm going to do is call him on the phone."

"I'll bet he doesn't say much on the phone," said Marsha. Her thick reddish hair had frizzed out in the Keys humidity, but the frizz looked good on her, made her seem less formal, looser, even playful. Light came through the edges of her hair and made her hazel eyes look brighter. "They never say much on the phone," she went on. "Not in the movies, at least. They don't trust the phone. Always want to meet in person."

"I don't think you should meet in person," said Sam. She wasn't wearing the desert commander hat that she wore on court but she still had that tone of quiet authority. "The people he deals with—just isn't worth the risk."

"If you do decide to meet him," Marsha put in, "don't go to his place. Whatever you do, don't go to his place." She said it in a level tone, but still, the words conjured images of ambush, thugs crouching in hallways with blunt objects, unconscious bodies being carried out and stuffed in car trunks. "Make sure it's in public at least."

Pat, more awake from moment to moment, her gray eyes gathering focus, said, "Aren't we getting a little ahead of ourselves? I'm only talking about a phone call."

Lenny put down the slice of honeydew he'd been nibbling. "Well, call him then. A dollar says he wants to meet in person."

Pat had a couple bites of a mango muffin, refreshed her coffee, and went into the house to try Bert's number. She was back outside in about two minutes. "He says we should meet in person," she announced.

"Figures," Marsha said. "Where?"

"His place."

Sam said, "But you didn't—"

"No, I didn't agree. I said I'd be more comfortable out in public. We settled on Smathers Beach an hour from now."

There was a brief pause then Lenny said, "All of us should go." He was a little surprised at himself for saying it, but, once he had, he had no choice but to continue. "Look, if it's a set-up, there'd probably be three of them. If we all go, that makes four of us. We'd have them outnumbered."

Marsha rolled her eyes. "Yeah, we'd be really intimidating."

"I'm just saying it seems safer. Anybody disagree?"

⚓ ⚓ ⚓

The patio of the Flagler House hotel was topped by a vine-draped trellis that broke the filtered sunlight into a pattern of stretched rectangles stamped with shapes of leaves. At a table cooled by squirts of mist from overhead spigots, Carmine was drinking a Bloody Mary and eating scrambled eggs. Through a mouthful of egg and toast, he said, "Ya know, there isn't one damn thing I like about this job."

Peppers was having an omelet with extra peppers in it, in this case jalapenos. He'd also shaken a bunch of pepper sauce on top, and now his skin was flushed from the spice, but the flush was more a dyspeptic yellow than a robust red. He said, "There hasn't been one damn thing you liked since we crossed the state line."

"And you know why?" the big man shot right back. "Because it's all been bullshit. The strip club, bullshit. Our local bigshot, a creep. Plus I really don't like it that the target's a woman. Plus now we got this old man who it takes him four minutes to say one simple thing and on top of that he's tryin' to run the show."

"That's a good thing," Peppers said, savoring the zing of his omelet, tingling with a light sweat in spite of the misters. Almost daintily, he dabbed some moisture from his hairline. "Less responsibility for us."

Carmine yanked the celery stalk from his glass and savagely bit into it. "Good thing," he mimicked. "Less responsibility. Fine. But don'tcha ever get sick of bein' bossed around? Bossed around by Lou. Bossed around by this little shit of a business guy. Now the fossil with the stupid little dog is actin' like our boss. Don'tcha ever just get sick of it?"

Peppers decided he simply wouldn't answer. He ate his omelet and kept his eyes down on his plate. Truth was, his buddy's endless pissing and moaning was finally wearing him down. It was exhausting always being the one to stay positive, to do the cheering up. So he just kept quiet.

Even Carmine could tell that the lack of a response was a kind of silent scolding. Feeling rebuked, he finished his drink and wagged his glass in the air to order another. When he'd slurped down half of it he started in again, but this time in a very different tone, quiet, almost sheepish. "Peps," he said, "can I ask you something, just totally, absolutely between the two of us?"

Softening in turn, the other man said, "Sure, Carmine. Sure."

The big guy lowered the angle of his neck and brought his voice down almost to a whisper. "Y'ever have a whaddyacallit, a hallucination? Like you see somethin' but it isn't there? Hear somethin' but there's nothin' to hear?"

"Ya mean, like, a fantasy, a daydream?"

"Nah, not really. It's more, I don't know...more exact. Like what you're hearing or seeing, there's only one thing it could be, except it isn't real."

Peppers just pushed his plate aside and looked at his friend.

"Just between us, right?"

Peppers nodded.

"The other night, at the club, just for this one crazy second, I thought I heard her laughing. I was sure of it."

Peppers didn't need to be told who he was talking about. He said, "Lots of people have nice laughs."

"Not like hers. It cut right through me. Can't get it out of my mind."

Peppers kept quiet for a moment, then said, "Carmine, she's fifteen hundred miles away. You know that, right?"

The big man paused and chewed his lip before finally nodding. "Yeah," he said. "I know it." He picked up his glass, put it down again without drinking from it, and kept his eyes on the patio's splotches of sun and shade. "Peps, listen, I know I've been a pain in the ass. I don't even know how to say I'm sorry for it. Can't even promise that it's gonna stop. I just want you to know I know, okay?"

"Okay," said Peppers. "Nice a you to say. Don't worry about it. You'll put this behind you, Carmine. I know you will."

30

"Jeez," said Bert, "I didn't expect ya'd bring a delegation."

He was sitting on Smathers Beach in an aluminum folding chair with yellow nylon webbing, wearing a cabana set in Kelly green terry-cloth and sunglasses with blue reflective lenses that perfectly matched the small pair that was perched on the nose of his dog.

"I was nervous coming alone," Pat admitted, though she felt a little sheepish saying it, considering that the beach was fairly crowded with women in thongs and young guys throwing footballs and even a few older people reading books.

"Ya don't trust me." This was not voiced as a question and Pat didn't answer it. "But okay, you're smart not to," the old man went on. "I'll take that as a compliment on my acting."

Pat said, "So the tough talk last night, you were faking it?"

"I had to."

At that, a feisty woman with sunlight streaming through her nimbus of reddish hair spoke up. "So how do we know you're not faking it now?"

"Excellent question and very *a propos*. I guess you don't. And who the hell, if I may make bold to ask, are you?"

"Marsha." Then, with a pride and conviction she hadn't let herself feel in quite a while, she added, "Lenny's wife."

"Ah, very nice. And who the hell is Lenny?"

"That would be me," he said.

"Oh yeah, the bartender who doesn't know how to make an Old-Fashioned. Hope you have a day job."

"Comedy writer."

"Guess I shoulda figured," the old man said. Then, shielding his eyes from the sharp glints off the ocean, he turned toward Sam. "And you, you look familiar. The tennis teacher, right? I've seen you in the park."

"Name's Sam."

"And this here is Nacho. And now that the introductions have been dispensed with, could I please ask youse to sit down? Sorry I can't offer chairs, but it's a little tough onnee the arthritis in my neck, lookin' up like this all day."

More or less in sync, the four of them dropped down onto the sand in a semicircle around him. The group now looked like an improv parody of a kindergarten class or a tableau from the ashram of an obscure sect being granted an audience with its guru. Bert said, "Okay, so let's start at the beginning. Last night, you thought I was the wingman for the pricks, pardon my French, who wanna take your club away. Am I right?"

Pat just nodded.

"So lemme tell you why I struck that pose or adopted that stratagem or however you wanna put it. I did it because it's the only way I could think of to have some influence and maybe help steer the situation away from some really bad things happening."

Lenny said, "Like what kind of things?"

"Better not t'ask. Nothing you'd find comical."

The seated people started squirming. Smathers was not a

comfortable beach to sit on, even without the threat of bad things happening. The top layer of sand barely covered the sharp nubs of coral that the Florida Keys were made of, and tormenting little arrowheads of rock were always poking upward into thighs and backsides.

Subtly shifting her position, Marsha said, "If it's really that bad, maybe we should contact the authorities."

"Here?" said Sam. She'd lived in Key West twenty years. "In this town? Against the bubbas? Please."

"Plus which," Bert put in, "it's not like anyone's done anything illegal yet. So it's like a whaddyacallit, a catch-22. Can't run to the cops until somethin' bad happens, and once it happens, what the hell can the cops do except draw that chalk outline onna floor? Sorry, I'm just speakin' figurative. But anyway, this is why we gotta handle it ourselves."

"Handle it *ourselves*?" murmured Lenny. The notion struck him as both terrifying and preposterous. *In the left-hand corner, an entrenched local bigshot and the Mob; in the right-hand corner, a geriatric, two comedy writers, a tennis coach, and an associate literature professor.* Not a bad set-up for a joke, maybe, but very unpromising for a battle.

Ignoring the dubious tone, Bert petted his dog and went on. "Look, forget about muscles and physiques and such. When it comes to dealin' wit' people like this, it's mostly a matter of understandin' their mentality. And I like to think we have an edge in the mentality department."

"I would certainly hope so," Marsha said.

Bert let that pass. "So look, when people like this want something, it usually starts off they want it for the money. But then it gets to be a game. So now they want it for two reasons. For the money and because they like to win and hate to lose. So it's very difficult, once they want something, to make them give up on having it. You with me so far?"

The people on the sand shifted and squirmed. No one said a word. Spent wavelets hissed at the water's edge. Kids kept throwing footballs.

"So basically," Bert went on, "there are several approaches to making them stop wanting something. One, let's call it the direct approach, is you make them feel that having this thing would not be worth the cost of getting it, because of, say, loss of manpower due to job-related injuries such as rubouts. I don't think that's the right approach for us."

"So glad we agree on that," said Pat.

"Another approach is what I think of as the-dog-with-the-pair-of-socks-and-piece-of-liver approach."

"Excuse me?" Marsha said.

"Like, you know the way some people like to roll their socks into a ball? Makes them very attractive to a dog. So the dog grabs the socks and is chewing them all to hell. The dog's having fun. But the guy wants his socks back. But he knows that if he just tries to grab 'em outa the dog's mouth, the dog'll think it's a tug a war and the socks'll be destroyed. So instead of doin' that, he lets the dog keep the socks but he dangles a piece of liver, too. *Capeesh?* He shows the dog something he wants even more than the socks, and the socks fall outa his mouth. Course, in real life, with real people, the hard part is comin' up with something they want even more than what they already think they want."

There was a pause. The heightening sun went from yellow to white and the day slipped seamlessly from warm to hot. A small plane flew by, trailing an ad banner. Lenny said, "Well, there's always Ricky."

Pat and Sam and Marsha glared at him.

Bert said, "Who's Ricky?"

Backpedalling, fending off disapproving looks from the faces all around him, Lenny said, "Nah, forget it. I was just being a jerk. Looking for a cheap laugh, some gallows humor."

The old man said, "Be that as it may, who's Ricky?"

Pat cleared her throat and said, "He's a friend of ours who your buddy Carmine wants to kill."

"Come again on that?"

"The guy who ran in naked the other night," the club owner explained. "You remember him, right?"

"How could I forget?"

"Well, his name's Ricky Reed and he bolted to Key West because, up in New York, he stole Carmine's girlfriend and Carmine has promised to cut his heart out."

"Up in New York?" Bert mused. "And now the both of 'em end up here?"

"Small world," said Lenny.

"And with a fair bit of lousy luck in it," Marsha added.

Bert took a moment to sift through all that. While he was sifting, he stroked his dog's head like he was stroking his own chin. Finally he said, "I'm not so sure it's a piece of lousy luck. Might actually be a break. Carmine wants to cut his heart out? That would suggest some strong emotion. Strong enough, maybe, to distract him from—"

"Now wait a second, Bert," said Pat. "Our friend Ricky is not a piece of liver. We're not going to dangle him—"

"Hol' on, hol' on," Bert interrupted in turn, raising a large and age-spotted hand. "No one's talkin' about danglin' anybody. But let's be realistic. What we got here is a ticklish situation. Ticklish for you. Ticklish for this Ricky guy. If we're gonna get through it, we gotta use what we can use. Like, whatever we can use. Can ya set me up a meeting with this Ricky?"

"Um, I don't know," Pat said. "I can ask. Not sure he'll do it. He's feeling a little bit paranoid."

"Paranoid, not paranoid, tell 'im to wear clothes. I don't sit down wit' naked guys. Make sure he unnerstands that. And inna meantime, I'd say we all got some good hard thinkin' to do."

31

At Kruzer King on Truman Avenue, two decidedly downmarket-looking tourists were trying to rent bicycles and making the transaction a lot more complicated than it needed to be. That was always the way, mused the clerk, who had grommets in his earlobes, studs through his lip, and who'd learned to pass the time at his incredibly boring job by making judgments about the different categories of customers who wandered in. He'd noticed that it was always the trashy ones, like these two, who hemmed and hawed about leaving a driver's license or credit card as collateral. The well-to-do, in their neat khakis and pastel polos—the ones whose Visa numbers and personal information might actually have been worth stealing—were always so blasé about putting their spending power and their identities into the hands of total strangers while they took a carefree spin around the island.

In any case, these scruffy-looking customers declined to leave ID. In a slow, thick Southern accent, the one who'd been doing the talking said, "Nah, ah don't b'lieve ah'd care to do that. Ah prefer cash money."

The clerk frowned at him, noticing the missing teeth, the dorky hat that looked like an upside-down flower pot with a chin strap, and the cheap mirror-lensed sunglasses that shot back broken prisms. He said, "If you leave cash, I'll have to put it in the safe and write out a receipt."

"Tha'd be fahne. We ain't in no hurry."

"But maybe the people behind you are."

"No they ain't. Not unless they's Yankees."

At that, the other would-be renter gave a low gruff chuckle. He was wearing a baggy sweatshirt with the sleeves hacked off at the elbows, cutoff jeans with loose strings dangling, and an Atlanta Braves baseball cap with the brim pulled very low.

Grumpily, the clerk took the cash and filled out the receipt and the trashy pair wobbled off on their blue beach cruisers. When they'd gone a block or so, Carla said, "Maybe you laid it on a little thick with the Southern accent."

Ricky said, "Did ah? Ah only got ta practice it but oncet."

"Maybe you could turn it off now."

"Ah guess. But gosh, sometahmes it's harder ta get outta character than inta it. Anyways, how you doin', Sugar? You doin' okay?"

"My boobs are feeling a little squished. Other than that I'm fine."

They pedaled through the jam-packed business district with its crush of bodies and roar of Harleys, then into a cozy but still cramped neighborhood of skinny residential streets whose sun-softened asphalt tugged like taffy at their tires. Low, small houses peeked out shyly from between rampant blocs of bougainvillea; leggy allamanda vines crawled up and over chain-link fences, their sinewy tendrils sealing off front yards. Closer to the ocean, the streets got wider, the houses bigger, the landscape more open; the sky itself seemed gradually to grow higher and more roomy, and by the time this burgeoning expansion of space reached its climax at the beach, with its limitless light and sparkling empty air stretching out forever, Carla was almost giddy with excitement and a kind of nameless letting go.

It wasn't until that moment that she fully realized how squeezed most of her life had been. Squeezed into small rooms under low ceilings back in Queens. Squeezed between glass counters under phony lighting at her job. Squeezed until recently into a stifling and airless relationship with a crazily jealous boyfriend. Well, she promised herself, she was just about through with feeling squeezed. True, for the moment she felt squeezed pretty tight by a paranoiac lover who needed a lot of coaxing and a disguise just to step outside the confines of their hotel room. But that wasn't the real Ricky; at least she hoped it wasn't. That was Ricky in crisis, understandably relentless in his self-involvement. Once the crisis had passed, the real Ricky would emerge...right? He'd be free of this fretful self-concern, ready to be a wonderful companion for travels and adventures and lots of laughs under lots of boundless skies. The prospect of those open skies overwhelmed her whispering doubts about the man she'd fallen in love with and made her so happy that she stood up on her pedals and barely felt the effort of making the wide tires spin.

⛴ ⛴ ⛴

The four-cheese calzone at Vinny's of Varick Street had a center like a volcano, and Fat Lou knew it was unwise to bite into it at the same moment he was dialing up a phone call. But he couldn't help himself. He was hungry and the vapors curling up from the calzone—garlic, oregano, fruity olive oil—were just too tempting.

So he took a chomp and burned his face four different ways. A whiplash of mozzarella unfurled and branded him on the chin. A clump of molten ricotta lodged in a tender spot between his lower lip and gums. The blue part of the gorgonzola sizzled down to fiery granules that seared his tongue. And the parmesan stuck to the roof of his mouth as though welded on with an arc lamp. "Fuck!" he said, just as Bert was picking up the landline in his kitchen.

"That's a fine way to start a conversation."

"Hol' on a minute. I just burned my mouth. I think it's gonna blister."

Bert waited. While he waited, he grabbed a dog treat from a cabinet and held it up in the air. The chihuahua jumped about three feet high and did a full three-sixty while grabbing it out of his fingers.

When Fat Lou came back on the line he seemed to be sucking an ice cube. It clattered against his molars. "I just had a call from Ted Clifton," he said.

"Lucky you."

"He's not real happy you're involved."

"Then my efforts haven't been in vain."

"Says you got a conflict of interest."

"He's right. I do."

"Says you're gumming up the works."

"Right again. I am."

"Wants me to take you off the job."

"Fine by me. Just say the word."

There was a pause. Fat Lou looked down at the steaming calzone with the big bite missing. He knew in his heart that it was still too hot to eat but he simply couldn't resist. The burn was only half as bad this time. When he was able to speak again, he said, "Bert, I don't see how we're gonna get anywhere if you just keep agreeing wit' everything I say."

"Sorry, but I ain't heard nothin' I disagree with yet." He winked at the dog. The dog ran around in little circles, paws ticking and skidding against the old linoleum. "But lemme ask you one now. This club owner whose lease you want. Clifton ever tell ya it's a woman?"

"A woman? No, he never mentioned that."

"And there you have it. Clifton in a nutshell. Allergic to the simple truth. Always holdin' somethin' back. Well, it so happens that your Galahads don't feel so great about roughin' up a woman."

"So don't rough her up. Don't even touch her. Leave 'er out of it altogether. Just torch her fuckin' place and have it over with."

"Fine. Great," said Bert. "'Cept it wouldn't be over with. It's city property, Lou. Ya don't think there'd be a long investigation? Could take years. City could end up condemning and then it'd be no use to anybody. Plus what if our bozo cops actually solve a case for once?

Who's left holdin' the gas can? Can you afford to send these guys on a long vacation in the slammer? So that's why I'm gummin' up the works. Tryin' to prevent people doin' somethin' dumb that they ain't thought through. But hey, it's your deal. You want me to step aside, say the word and I'm gone."

Lou had gone back to his calzone while Bert was talking. It was a pretty perfect temperature by now, hot enough to send fragrant steam wafting up his sinuses, not so hot as to further aggravate his scalded taste buds. He wiped his oily lips on a paper napkin then dropped it onto a pile of several others he'd already gone through. Finally he said, "Okay, Bert, I hear what you're sayin', but can you try and meet me halfway, at least? Can ya be a little nicer to Clifton? Can ya show 'im some respect?"

"No. Now you're askin' me to do something that I cannot do."

"Try to keep him a little happier?"

"I don't want 'im to be happy."

"Try to keep him off my back at least?"

"Okay, fair enough, that much I think I can do. Don't know exactly how, but I'll get him off your back."

32

"You want me to do *what?*" said Ricky. "With *who?*"

They'd been pedaling against a warm east breeze almost to the end of the oceanfront promenade and were way up by the airport when his phone rang. The incoming number was Pat's, so he hit the brakes and took the call. Carla stepped off her cruiser and leaned it on its kickstand, then sat down on the knee-high seawall, lightly kicking her heels against it like a little kid. Below, in maybe six inches of water, baby barracudas were darting out of shadows and gobbling other fishes' babies. Small rays stirred plumes of silt as they hoovered up unlucky shellfish from the bottom.

"You trust him?" Ricky was saying to his phone. "Oh, you *think* you trust him. That's just swell. The old gangster hangs around in clubs with the guy who wants to kill me, but you're pretty sure he's on our side. Pretty sure. What if you're pretty wrong? I guess that makes me pretty dead."

At the waterline, the seawall was studded with barnacles that gleamed like onyx. Carla watched as crabs with outstretched claws strained upwards toward them, trying to gain a purchase on their shells so they could crush them and suck their insides out. Gulls hovered and squawked, grabbing some of the slower crabs then dropping them from a great height to smash their bodies on the pavement.

Ricky said, "I don't care if it's public and crowded, I don't want to meet him on the beach. I don't want to meet him anywhere. He scares me, okay?...Yeah, I know he's a very old man. He scares me anyway, what can I say?"

Carla looked on as, a few yards away, a heron skewered a fish right through the middle. Farther offshore, an osprey tucked its wings and swooped, then flew away with its wriggling prey clasped in pitiless talons.

Ricky said, "You think it's maybe our best chance to get this settled? Get *what* settled?...The club? They're trying to take the club away? Shit, I'm sorry for that, but look, everyone has troubles. Most aren't fatal. Some are...Yeah, I know I'm being selfish. Trying to survive does that to people."

A pelican dove. A heartbeat later, Carla saw the outlines of doomed sardines writhing in its throat sac. A tern skimmed the roiled water and picked off one that got away.

Ricky held the phone a little distance from his ear, closed his eyes as if avoiding the sight of some disaster, and frowned. Finally, with a theatrical sigh, he said, "All right, all right. I'll meet with him, but only under one condition. Only if it's at your house, and if you and Lenny are there, and if you guys scout the street and make sure he arrives alone...Okay, okay you're right, that's three conditions. Don't be so fucking literal. I'll see you there in an hour."

He clicked out of the call and put the phone back in his pocket. Carla tore herself away from the various murders she'd been watching and got back on her bike. The breeze was behind them as they pedaled back toward town.

⚓ ⚓ ⚓

Marsha and Lenny were standing in the pool. It was that part of afternoon when the sun was sliding along in a perfect groove between the palms so that shadows danced around the edges of the yard but never fell across the water. Marsha was wearing a chaste two-piece with polka dots that she hadn't put on since the previous Labor Day at Fire Island. Her shoulders and tummy were very pale, as pale as Lenny's had been just a few days earlier, the kind of pale that showed tan lines in about five minutes. She was doing some gentle aerobics, slowly swinging her arms against the resistance of the outflow from the skimmer. Tiny water droplets twinkled on the ends of her hair. Now and then one broke loose and tickled the back of her neck. "I see why you love it here," she said in mid-exercise. "But did you really have to just run off like that?"

"Yeah, I did," said Lenny, who was folding himself over the pool steps, trying to stretch out a balky hamstring. "Sorry. It wasn't planned. Didn't really know what I was doing. But I guess I had to. If I stuck around we would have just kept arguing, digging in. Nothing good would have come of it."

"I was being pretty tough on you," she said.

"I deserved it. I was in a bad rut. Knew I was but couldn't climb out. Didn't like the way I was acting, the way I was sounding. Pretending nothing could really bother me as long as I could make a dumb joke out of it. Nothing against dumb jokes. My bread and butter. I just got a little too relentless about it."

"And I went way too far the other way," admitted Marsha. "Started sounding like a total killjoy. It's weird—you stake out a position and suddenly you hear yourself saying things you don't really believe. Or half-believe, at most. And saying them solemnly. Like, how dare anybody laugh with the shape the world is in? Well, who the hell am I—who the hell is anybody—to tell people whether it's okay to laugh or not? I don't blame you for getting sick of hearing it."

He shrugged that off and began trying with very little result to stretch out the other hamstring. "Kind of funny," he said, "that we had to come to the goofiest town in the world to sort of be reminded what's serious and what isn't."

"And that being a goofball isn't the worst thing a person could be."

"So you still think I'm a goofball?"

"Yeah, pretty much. I wouldn't have it any other way."

33

Ted Clifton looked up from some papers on his immaculately polished desk in his mock-authentic office and said, "Generally, Bert, I only see people by appointment."

"Duly noted. But I was in the neighborhood and thought I'd stop by anyway." He sat down across from his host without waiting for an invitation and unceremoniously plopped his chihuahua down onto a corner of the faultless desk. The fastidious businessman frowned at the dog and wondered what sort of unsavory things it might have been rolling in lately. Bert said, "Fat Lou tells me you're very unhappy with me."

Clifton flushed around the collar and fished for words that didn't come. It was clear he hadn't expected his complaints to be passed along.

"A very straightforward guy, Fat Lou," the old man went on. "I like that in a person. The opposite of straightforward, that I don't admire too much. Anyways, I thought I'd check in with a progress report."

"So?"

"The report is that there's very little and that if you keep gettin' in Lou's face and bitching about me behind my back there's gonna be even less. That's the bad news. The good news is that there is some slight but meaningful progress. Pat Coates understands the situation. She gets it that the goombahs aren't just decorative. She's considering her options."

Smugly and impatiently, Clifton said, "She has no options."

"No good options, maybe. But she has a couple choices. She can cave and try to cut a deal, or she can say fuck you and call our bluff. So far she's leaning toward fuck you."

"That'll change when you stop wasting time and show her that you aren't bluffing."

"We," said Bert.

"Excuse me?"

"That *we* aren't bluffing. You and Lou are partners, Ted. You seem to forget that at convenient moments. Lou is not your hired help and Lou's guys are not your hired help. It's a partnership. If our bluff gets called and if a line gets crossed, if someone gets hurt, someone dies, you're just as responsible as anybody else. Aren't you even man enough to admit that to yourself?"

It was impossible to tell if it was the comment that finally shook Clifton out of his bland and almost clinical composure, or if it was that the dog, at that moment, curled itself into an arc on a Morocco leather corner of his desk blotter and began noisily licking its anus and the blank pink place where its balls had been, then nuzzling its damp and soiled nose back and forth against some papers. In any case, the businessman abruptly pushed back in his rolling chair, sprang up into a belligerent and exasperated forward lean, puffed out his purplish cheeks, and violently shoved the dog off the desk. The little creature flew off the polished edge as if it were a ski jump, did two back flips and a half-twist in mid-air, its paws seeming to rotate in slow-motion like the panels of a satellite, then landed, flailing, in its master's lap. It gave one quick whimper then started licking Bert's fingers as though nothing at all had happened.

The old man looked sorrowfully at his host's engorged and twitching face. "And now you're pickin' on a three-pound dog. Really, Ted, you oughta be ashamed."

ONE BIG JOKE

Alone in the small, low-ceilinged, and very air-conditioned fitness room at the Flagler House hotel, Carmine was lifting weights. There were many pleasanter things to do on a perfect Key West winter afternoon, but the big man seemed to have no interest in doing any of them. So he stayed indoors and by himself, lifting dumbbells and barbells, kettle bells and stacks of iron plates attached to cables, lifting anything that was there to be lifted. His expression hardly changed as he raised the weights and put them down again. He didn't grunt or groan. There was a grim steadiness, an unwavering and unpunctuated tempo in how he lifted, as if the lifting were an act of penance or ritual of mourning.

The fitness room had mirrored walls, and although, in the past, Carmine had taken pride in watching his torso swell and his arm muscles tighten into ropes as he worked out, today he tried to avoid seeing his own reflection. When he did catch a glimpse of himself, he didn't much like what he saw. A bulky man of great strength but little grace; a fierce but aimless figure sweating alone in an empty gym.

He kept lifting. He added more weight, more repetitions, until at some point he began to feel lightheaded. The sensation was not totally unpleasant, less like dizziness than a kind of swimming in the air. While he was feeling it, he bent to put some weights back in their rack, and when the bar settled lightly into its cradle it gave off an unexpected ping, a tinkling sound of a certain volume and particular pitch, and Carmine once again heard a brief note of Carla laughing. It struck him as the most welcome but also the most unwelcome sound in the world. If the sound pursued him even to an empty gym in a faraway town, where did he have left to hide?

There was a punching bag in the gym, the old-fashioned kind that was filled with sand and hung from the ceiling by a heavy chain. He went over and hit it as hard as he could. The bag recoiled and the chain rang with that same certain note. In a fury now, he swung at the bag again and again, making it twirl in a widening loop while the chain mercilessly squeaked out its softly maddening music. He punched until he could barely lift his arms, then he leaned exhausted into the bag of sand and held it against himself for some moments in a mockery of an embrace. In those moments, with his chest pounding against the lifeless bundle, he finally understood something that he hadn't quite let himself believe before, not really. Carla was never coming back to him. It didn't matter what he did or didn't do, who else was or wasn't in between them. It was over. She was lost. He finally got it. When he killed her lover, it wouldn't be with any lame imagining that he could once again reclaim his place. It would only be to punish her. To punish her for haunting him. And maybe to make the mocking laughter finally stop.

Embarrassed by how long he'd stood there numbly in the clinch, he pushed the bag away with fresh rage and started pummeling it again, telling himself it was only sweat that flew from the corners of his eyes as he whaled on it.

34

Pat and Lenny were, as promised, patrolling Pine Street when Bert came walking slowly up the lane that led from Bayview Park. "Hey," he said, "ya didn't have ta come out to meet me. I woulda found the house."

"We're on guard duty," Lenny said. "Making sure your buddies didn't tag along."

"Ricky insisted," said Pat apologetically. "He's afraid of you."

Without nostalgia, Bert said, "Been a long time since anybody felt that way. But, nah, it's just me and the dog. Unarmed. Wanna frisk me? I could use a little thrill."

The offer went untaken and the three of them strolled into the perfect yellow house then straight through it to return to daylight by the pool. Near its edge, in a patch of shade, Marsha was reading in a lounge chair. Sam was stringing a racquet on a machine she'd set up by the pump shed. On the table was a bucket full of wine bottles. Pat poured drinks and for a couple minutes everyone made rather labored small talk.

Then, from the narrow, tangled side yard, there came sounds of twigs snapping, vines being torn, creepers getting yanked out of the ground. Muffled curses and metallic squeaks were added to the complaints of slaughtered vegetation before the gate swung open and Ricky and Carla rolled in on their rented cruisers, whose spokes and chains were fouled with shreds of weed and whose fenders trailed festoons of greenery. Bits of leaf and a few twisting caterpillars were sticking to their clothes. To the questioning eyes of the others, Ricky said, "I thought it would be safer, staying in the foliage."

Introductions were made. Bert said to Ricky, "What happened to your teeth?"

"Oh shit, I forgot to take this out." He reached into his mouth and removed the plastic shield that had blacked out a few canines and incisors. He swept off the goofy-looking flower-pot hat and the cheap mirror shades, and quickly turned into just a normal person. "Minimal disguise," he said.

"Not as minimal as the one I saw you in the first time," answered Bert. Then he looked with some confusion at Ricky's companion. From what he'd heard, he imagined she must be a real *femme fatale,* but she just appeared to be a skinny guy in a baseball cap. "And you must be Carla."

She reached out a hand and he saw the long red nails. She swept off the cap and shook free her lush black hair. Then she asked Pat if she could slip inside a moment and take off the tight tube-top that was practically strangling her. When she returned, Bert understood things a little better.

The seven of them plus the dog squeezed in around the poolside table that was really meant for four. Knees touched. Shoulders swiveled to make room. Bert sipped some wine and said, "Okay, someone's gotta start the meeting. So, first question. Why are we here? We're here because youse got a problem. Actually, as I understand it, youse got two problems, which, doing the math, I surmise is twice as bad as having one. Question is, which problem do we look at first?"

Without hesitation, Pat said, "Ricky's. I mean, his problem is serious. Mine's just stuff, just my club."

Bert petted his chihuahua while, with the other hand, he raised a yellowish, Socratic finger. "Agreed that Ricky's problem is more serious, as in fatal. But onnee other hand, the scumbag who wants your club is breathin' down my neck to get it done, whereas, if I understand correctly, the guy who wants to eliminate Ricky doesn't even know that Ricky is in town. So, by that criteria or let's say yardstick, the Titters problem is actually more pressing."

"Great," said Ricky, "so I'm supposed to take a number and wait in line like at the freakin' deli?"

"Don't get touchy. You'll get your turn."

Just then Lenny's phone rang. The tone sounded very loud at the crowded table in the otherwise quiet yard. He glanced at the screen and said, "Sorry, I have to take this." He looked sideways at Pat. "It's Morty." Then he quickly slipped away from the table.

Bert said, "Who the hell is Morty?"

"His agent," said Pat.

The old man couldn't help feeling slightly miffed about that. "I'm talkin' life and death heah, and he takes a call from his agent?"

"Obviously you've never worked in the entertainment industry," said Marsha.

In thirty seconds Lenny was back, a little breathless. "Morty spoke with the suits. Says we have three days. If we can get back to New York by Monday, we can still shoot the pilot."

Bert said, "Who the hell's the pilot?"

"He means the show we were working on together before this whole craziness got started," said Pat.

"Ah. So it's a professional opportunity. A big one, I take it. An incentive to get stuff figured out."

"I thought," said Carla, "that keeping Ricky alive might be incentive enough."

"Never hurts to have some extra," Bert opined. "Plus a deadline. Deadline's good. Focuses the mind. Um, okay, where the hell were we?"

"You were just telling me," said Ricky, "that my little problem is second in line."

"Will you please let go a that? Look, when the guy who wants to ice you figures out you're here, your problem will shoot straight to number one. Now ya happy?"

Happy is not how Ricky looked. He reached into the bucket and poured himself more wine.

Carla said, "The way I see it, if Carmine realizes Ricky's here, Pat catches a break. At least for a while. I mean, the man's obsessed with getting back at Ricky. The club thing, it's just a job. And the guy is not a multi-tasker, trust me. So if he's gotta choose between his obsession or a gig, the gig is gonna wait."

"Which would really piss off the little business creep, right?" said Lenny. "He's all hot to get the club. Does he even know about the bad blood with the boyfriends? And if he does know, why the hell would he care? Him and Carmine, their priorities are exactly opposite."

Sam said, "Sounds kind of like a losing doubles game to me."

Bert's head had been flicking around toward each of the speakers in turn, and the quick movements had made his eyeballs dance around a bit. Now he tried to focus in on Sam and said, "Excuse me, I think I missed something. A doubles game? Like, tennis? Like, now we're talking tennis?"

"I'm just trying to boil all this down to something I understand," she said. "To me, it sounds like the guy who wants the club and the guy who wants revenge are supposedly on the same side but they're not really playing as a team. And if they're not playing as a team, then there should be ways to beat them."

Bert rubbed his dog's head while he considered that.

Ricky rolled his eyes. "Look, these sports analogies are very entertaining but can we please get back to me not getting murdered?"

"Hang on a sec," said Bert. "I'm likin' this. So if they're not really playing as a team…"

"Then it's usually possible," said Sam, "to get someone out of position."

"Jesus Christ," said Ricky. "My life is on the line and we're babbling away like fucking ESPN when there's no game on."

Ignoring the comment, Bert said softly, "Gettin' someone outa position. I think maybe we're onta somethin' heah. Somethin' to work with. Could be a start, at least."

He rubbed his dog between the ears. Pat poured out more wine. Afternoon shadows in the shapes of overlapping fronds began to stretch across the little yard, a soft breeze came up from the south, and shallow blue ripples chased each other across the surface of the pool.

35

"Where's Bert?" asked Peppers, as he and Carmine were being ushered into Ted Clifton's too tidy and too perfect office.

"He won't be joining us today," the businessman announced in a blasé and even dismissive tone as he gestured toward a pair of matching chairs on the far side of his desk. "But please, sit down."

"Why ain't he here?" pressed Carmine as he settled his bulk into the seat. His chest and shoulders were still pumped up from his workout and his shirt bound him in the armpits. His muscles ached and he liked it that they ached.

Clifton didn't answer right away. Instead, he reached into a drawer and produced a box of cigars. "Have one? Partagas. Cuban. The best. Still made in the traditional way. Rolled on the thighs of beautiful women. I hope you have a taste for them. Cigars, I mean. There could be a lot of these in your future."

The goombahs each took one. Their host clicked open an alabaster lighter and they stretched their necks out toward the flame. After they'd taken the first appreciative puff, Clifton said, "I thought it might be useful to have a talk just the three of us. In confidence, of course."

Peppers squinted through the blue smoke he'd just exhaled. "In confidence, like, from Bert? That makes me a little bit uncomfortable."

"Uncomfortable? Why? It's not like I'm asking you to do anything against the wishes or interests of your boss."

"Then why the secret meeting?" Carmine asked, propping a meaty elbow on the desk.

Clifton tried to smile at that. "It's not a secret meeting. It's a private meeting. There's a difference."

"There are also similarities," Peppers pointed out. "Like for example not everyone's invited and the guy who isn't invited isn't supposed to know it happened."

Clifton crinkled an eyebrow and said, "All right, fair enough. Look, I'll be candid. Brutally candid. Please don't take offense. This ancient friendship between Bert and Mr. Benedetti, it's very sweet, their loyalty is touching. But Mr. Benedetti seems to have no idea how much his old pal has declined. He still thinks of him as with it, even shrewd. Please. The fact is, he's a doddering old self-important busybody who's making everything way more complicated than it needs to be and opening up way more opportunities for something to go wrong."

Peppers puffed on his cigar and worked at pretending to like it more than he actually did. "Okay," he said, "that's your opinion. And who knows, maybe you're right. Jury's out. Be that as it may, Fat Lou told us Bert's in charge. Told us do things like Bert says."

Swallowing back frustration, Clifton said, "I understand. But why did Mr. Benedetti do that? Because Mr. Benedetti, who is very far away and probably hasn't seen his decrepit, rambling, meddling colleague in twenty years, thought it would be best. Except it isn't turning out like that, is it?"

The question hung for a moment among the wisps and whorls of smoke. The goombahs couldn't bring themselves to disagree.

"Look," the businessman went on, "I'm sure you have lives you'd like to get back to, and you're just as eager to wrap this up as I am. So the reason I asked you here today is to try and streamline the process. Better for me, better for you. Better for Mr. Benedetti also, even if he doesn't yet realize it. So here's my suggestion. A little side-deal. I will pay each of you ten grand in cash to step up and handle this the way it should be handled. Ignore the old man. Humor him. Whatever you think best. But one way or other, get it done."

Carmine said, "You're bribin' us to go against our boss?"

"Bribing? No. Absolutely not. I'm offering you a bonus to do what your boss wants anyway, but do it in a way that I prefer."

"That bears a certain similarity to a bribe," said Peppers.

"Look, it doesn't get us anywhere to sit here and argue the fine points of the English language. I'm offering you an extra payday. You interested or not?"

Peppers looked at Carmine. Carmine said, "You still ain't told us exactly what it is you'd be paying us to do."

Clifton flinched then rubbed his hands together in a kind of zig-zag pattern, like he was washing them in a public restroom. "That's your area of expertise, not mine."

Peppers said, "We ain't roughin' up a woman. We tol' you that already."

"And no one's asking you to do that."

There was a silent standoff. Peppers stopped faking enjoyment of his big cigar and put it in an ashtray. Carmine's was clenched between his teeth and his arms were crossed in a way that challenged the seams of his shirt. Finally giving in to simmering exasperation, Clifton went on, "Look, how you do the job is up to you. None of my business. But here's a piece of information. I don't need that fucking houseboat, okay? All I need's the dock space, the frontage. That fucking tub is blown to kingdom come, it's all one to me. Maybe you should keep that in mind while you consider my offer."

36

Carla was lingering in the shower. She'd already washed the residue of salt air from her skin, already shampooed and conditioned her hair, already shaved her legs. Now she was just standing there under the stream of hot water, letting it hammer down on the nape of her neck. Back in Queens, she'd seldom been allowed the luxury of such long and lazy showers; either the hot water would run out or another family member would be clamoring to use the bathroom. So here at the hotel she savored the endless supply of wet warmth and the rich steam that billowed up around her.

And, though she tried not to admit it to herself, she was savoring something else as well; she was savoring a little break from Ricky, stealing a little privacy, a little solitude...But wait, she wondered as the almost scalding water cascaded down between her shoulder blades: Why did it have to feel like stealing? Why should she feel guilty about taking a few extra minutes for herself? Was that just how she was, a dutiful, unselfish Catholic girl? Or was Ricky somehow putting that guilt on her, making her feel that even the smallest things she did for herself were things she was depriving him of? And if he was making her feel that way, why the hell was she letting him?

Eventually she came out of the bathroom with a robe on and a towel wrapped around her head. Ricky was sitting in front of the dresser mirror making faces at himself, practicing impressions of famous people.

"Okay, who am I doing?" he asked, as he puffed out his lips, stretched them into something like a spastic yawn, and spat out a couple words in an abrasive Cockney accent.

"That's what's-his-name, the really old guy with the band. Mick Jagger."

"Right. Too easy." He eased out of the rocker pose and now sat very still with his hands placidly folded and a rather smug expression on his face. "Okay, how 'bout this one?"

"I have no idea." She perched lightly on the edge of the bed. "Ricky, how long we been together now?"

Without looking up from the mirror, he said, "Hm? I dunno, a month or so? You really can't tell who this one is?"

"No. I can't."

"Stephen Colbert."

"He just looks like an average white guy."

"Exactly. It's subtle." He lowered his chin a quarter of an inch, trying to get closer to what made Colbert look like Colbert.

"Ricky, you think you know me pretty well?"

"Yeah, pretty well. Sure."

"I don't feel like I know you very well. I know you're funny. I don't really know much else."

He didn't answer that, just kept working toward a more perfect version of Colbert's snarky deadpan, which seemed to start with a slow and shallow lift of one eyebrow.

She unwound the towel from her hair and lightly rubbed her scalp with the dry side of it. "I sometimes wonder if we know each other well enough."

Now he was trying to get the curl of his lips exactly right. "Well enough for what?"

"Well enough, you know, to really believe we can make a go of it together."

He didn't look up. He finally thought he had it. The trick was in smiling with the teeth while smirking with the eyes alone. He said, "Sure we can. Of course we can. Why not?"

She shrugged and went off to dry her hair. He wiped the Colbert expression off his face and started doing Jimmy Kimmel. That one always got a laugh.

🌴 🌴 🌴

At Titters, Pat and Lenny and Marsha were sharing the dull but comforting afternoon chores that paved the way for every evening of triumph or disaster at the club. Replacing chairs around the tables. Tapping fresh kegs of beer. Testing microphones and mopping last night's sweat from the corners of the stage. When the place had been made as presentable as it was going to get, they sat down for a drink, though the mood was hardly festive. As they clinked glasses, Pat said, "Well, here's hoping we win one out of three, at least."

"One out of three?" said Marsha.

"Keeping Ricky alive. Keeping the club alive. Keeping *Dog Groomer* alive. All things considered, if we win on one out of three I'd say we're doing good."

"Nice spin," said Lenny, "but if we win one, we lose two, and that would suck. Even losing one would kind of suck. You know what wouldn't suck? Hitting the trifecta. That wouldn't suck."

Marsha said, "Ever the optimist. Ever the dreamer. Then he wonders why he's always disappointed and ends up in a funky mood."

"Maybe not this time," he protested.

There was a silence, long enough for the three of them to notice that the club smelled different before people started bringing in their scents of after-shave and residue of suntan lotion. Empty, it smelled like the ocean, or at least like a shallow, sluggish corner of it, with a hint of dry shells and rotting seaweed and just a whiff of diesel.

Finally Pat said, "Beating these guys, I just don't see how we could pull it off."

"Probably not," said Lenny. "But I do have kind of an idea. Well, okay, more like a piece of an idea."

He stopped talking and went back to his drink.

His wife said, "You can't just leave us hanging, Lenny. What's the idea?"

He gave a half-shrug and a half-shake of his head. "I dunno. Maybe I shouldn't even say it. Maybe it's just really dumb."

"Never stopped you before," said his sometime writing partner.

"Okay, okay. It's sort of a hybrid between what Bert was saying about the socks and the liver and what Sam was saying about playing doubles."

It was clear from the women's expressions that they had no idea where he was going with this. He didn't have much of one himself. But he sprang up from his chair and started pacing, leaning forward from both waist and neck.

"Okay, here's what I got so far. The socks and liver part: If we want to distract the goombahs from hassling you about the club, we have to let them find out Ricky's in town. But if we want to keep Ricky alive, we have to set it up so they can't just go right out and kill him. Which brings us to the playing doubles part: We have to make sure they go chasing after him, which will get them out of position."

"Out of position for what?" asked Marsha.

"How the hell should I know? I've gotta figure out everything? Whatever they were in position for before."

Pat said, "Maybe let's back up a step. Letting the bad guys know Ricky's in Key West. Just how do we manage that?"

He blinked at her. "You really need to ask? Shit, that's the easy part. That part's obvious."

"Not to me," said Pat.

He gestured toward the low and unlit stage. "Look, here we are in a comedy club. A public venue. With witnesses. And a back door to escape through. So we have Ricky do a show here, and we make sure the goombahs are in attendance."

Pat thought it over, not for long. "A show? Here? No. It's the worst idea I ever heard."

Lenny sat down again, elbows propped on knees, head sagging, his voice deflated. "I offered not to say it. You guys goaded me into saying it. Then you say it stinks."

"Ricky would never go for it," Pat said. "He won't even come out of his room except in a spacesuit or shepherd's garb or something. Now we're going to put him up on stage?"

"He's always on stage," said Marsha. "This would just be making it official. If we could just keep him safe—"

But Lenny was already souring on his own idea. "If we could keep him safe we'd be the Secret Service. Except we're not. We're not even the Postal Service. We're not even service dogs. Pat's right. He wouldn't do it, and he shouldn't. Way too risky."

"But if he *doesn't* do it," Marsha said, "if we don't try *something*, the threat just keeps hanging over him, and over the club, and the TV deadline comes and goes, and we've lost without even trying to win. I think putting Ricky up there front and center is a pretty damn good approach. Gets bodies in motion. Forces the issue."

"That's what I'm afraid of," said Pat.

"I think it's worth a shot, at least," said Marsha. "So, Lenny, you'll go talk to him?"

"Me? Why me?"

"It was your idea," said Pat. "You sort of own it now. Good luck."

PART FOUR

37

"I dunno," Carmine said as he sipped a Mai-Tai underneath a palapa at the Flagler House's outdoor bar. "Doin' an end-run around Bert, it just seems sorta, whaddyacallit, disrespectful."

Peppers took a swig of his Tabasco-spiked martini. "Ain't disrespectful if the guy never finds out he's been disrespected. Besides, we get this done neat and tidy, it would get us in good with Clifton."

"Who cares?"

"Maybe you should. Future opportunities down here—"

The big man was already shaking his head. Then he pointed up at the palapa, which he'd noticed was a fake. You were supposed to believe it was made of thatch, but if you looked close you could see it was really plastic. "Don't talk to me about opportunities in Florida. Florida's bullshit."

"All right," his friend continued, "leave that onna side for now. But ten grand is ten grand. An' all Clifton's askin' us to do, it's probably where things end up anyway. Plus we don't have to beat up the broad."

"Look, I just don't feel right takin' Fat Lou's money to do a job then takin' someone else's money to do the job different."

"As long as it gets done," argued Peppers, "what's wrong with a little double-dippin'? Waya the world, my friend."

Carmine folded his arms across his chest and thought it over. Then he said, "Tell ya what, let's compromise."

"Compromise?"

"We do like Clifton wants but not wit'out we get Bert's blessing."

"Bert's blessing? Oh, great. We just tell 'im we've decided to ignore 'im—"

"No, we level with 'im altogether. We tell 'im we got a chance to take some money off this guy who it's obvious he hates his guts. We tell 'im we're sick a sittin' on our ass down here. And we tell 'im this is what we'd like to do."

"And what if he says no?"

"Then we don't do it."

"So we leave the money onna table and go back to sittin' on our ass?"

"No worse off than now." He sipped his drink. When it got near the bottom he sucked the rest up through a straw. He knew his partner wasn't thrilled with him, but what else was new? Finally he said, "Listen, Peps. I done a lotta wrong things in my life. I'm probably gonna do a lot more before I'm through. But bein' a sneak wit' my own people ain't one of 'em. I'm not doin' this unless we clue Bert in."

⚓ ⚓ ⚓

Ricky was still mugging for the mirror when the unexpected knock came at the door.

The sound made the hunted man's heart start racing and his first impulse was to hide in the closet or leap from the balcony and take his chances with the shrubbery below. Even after Lenny had announced himself, it took a few moments for his breathing to return to normal. He unlocked the door three different ways and let him in.

After some terse hellos, Lenny got straight to the point. "I have a hypothetical question for you. How'd you like to do a set at Titters, maybe, for instance, tomorrow night? With some Mafia in the audience."

Ricky blinked and said, "And I have a hypothetical question for you. Are you fuckin' nuts?"

Carla came out of the bathroom. She'd been giving herself a pedicure and had those foam toe-separating thingies on both feet. They made her walk like a duck. She said, "Did I hear right? You want Ricky up on stage with Carmine in the room?"

"Exactly."

Ricky said, "And I'm supposed to stand there and be funny?"

"That's your job, right? You're a pro, you can do it. Lighten up, rise above. Have some fun with it."

"Fun. Right."

Carla said, "So I'm trying to picture all this. The show happens. Then what?"

Lenny couldn't hold anybody's gaze just then so he looked down at Carla's toes and quietly said, "Well, um, the idea from there is that Carmine probably freaks and goes chasing after Ricky but Ricky makes a getaway."

"A getaway," said the comedian. "How quaint. How vintage. How *Bonnie and Clyde*. Just how the hell does this getaway happen?"

"Um, we don't really know that yet. We just know we have to get Carmine out of position."

"Oh, Christ, we're back to fucking tennis strategy again?"

"Maybe we just hide you someplace."

"*Someplace? Maybe?* This is the most half-assed thing I've ever heard."

"Come on, man, you've done improv, you know how to wing it."

"Yeah, when the worst that can happen is no one laughs and you feel like an idiot. This is, like, if it falls flat, my testicles are gone."

There was a pause. Unconsciously, the three of them had been gradually leaning inward toward each other, so that by now their bodies formed a kind of teepee; the fumes from Carla's toenail polish were wafting up between them like toxic incense from a campfire.

Finally she said, "Look, worse comes to worst, I'll handle Carmine."

"You'll handle Carmine? Oh, great. Wonder Woman to the rescue." Ricky's tone wasn't exactly mocking but it was skeptical enough to come close.

"Your confidence in me is touching," Carla said, pivoting away from the group and taking a few huffy steps toward the balcony. The dramatic effect of this was somewhat reduced by the fact that she was still walking like a duck.

Backpedaling, Ricky said, "Look, no offense, but what if Carmine just doesn't feel like being handled? What if he's crazy enough to kill you too?"

"He had plenty of chance to do that when I told him I was leaving him. He didn't do it then. I don't think he'll do it now."

"You're really not afraid of him?"

"For myself? No. But that's fine. You're afraid enough for both of us. Besides, I'd actually like to have a little chat with Carmine. There's a couple things I'd like to say to him."

"A chat? How cozy. How civilized. I hope its cathartic for you. I hope it's therapeutic for you both. But if it doesn't exactly clear the air, I'm still the one with the bull's-eye on my chest."

They were glaring at each other, hands on hips. Lenny, unwilling witness to the private spat, eased back into the conversation on a different tack. "Ricky, how long's it been since you were up on stage? You know, live audience. Not counting the naked gate-crash."

"Months."

"Miss it?"

"You know I do."

"You'll be missing it a whole lot longer if you keep on hiding out. I think maybe you should face this thing while you've got friends around, people who can help."

Ricky pushed his lips out and stared down at the carpet. He pawed at it a moment and watched the nap rise and fall. Then, belatedly, he said to Carla, "What kind of things you want to say to Carmine?"

"That's between him and me. Maybe they'll help, maybe they won't. But in the meantime, I think you ought to do the show."

38

"Fuckin' circus down here," said Carmine.

"Well yeah," said Bert. "That's kinda the idea."

The three of them and the chihuahua were milling through the crowd at Mallory Square, where the fabled Sunset Celebration was in full swing. There were jugglers, tightrope walkers, acrobats, steel drums. Painted people pretended to be statues and a mime made you see a wall made out of nothing. People were crushed together and it was sometimes hard to tell the buskers from the spectators, what with the tats and piercings and zombie eye makeup common to both groups. Peppers thought it was a helluva place for a meeting on delicate matters, but Bert had insisted that's where they should get together. He thought the visitors might momentarily lighten up and enjoy it, plus he liked to shmooze with the performers, most of whom seemed to know him well.

So they wandered among the guitarists and magicians and guys up on stilts. Peppers, at moments, caught himself almost having fun but Carmine remained resolutely stone-faced. Not even the famous cats that leaped from ladder to ladder through hoops of bright green flame seemed to impress him. "Ain't they somethin'?" Bert coaxed.

"They're okay," Carmine said warily and without enthusiasm. In his limited exposure to Florida attractions, he'd already noted a pattern of fraud. Places with strip club names that turned out not to be strip clubs;

Polynesian tiki huts that featured plastic fronds. He was tired of feeling suckered. "That fire they're jumpin' through," he groused, "I'll bet it's not even real fire."

"Not real fire? Whaddya want, napalm? Ya wanna see the cats get fried? You want a barbecue? Course it's real fire, same kind fire-eaters eat. We got one a those too. Wanna see 'im eat fire?"

"Not really," said the big man.

"Look, Bert," said Peppers, "no offense against your freak show, but what we'd really like to do is discuss some pressing business. Can we please leave the carnival and talk?"

Bert just shrugged and led the way toward a relatively quiet place where a cruise ship had steamed off, leaving a long stretch of empty concrete dock. He put Nacho on the ground and let the creature choose which giant bollard it preferred to pee on. Then he carefully sat himself down on one nearby. "Okay, what's the pressing business?"

Peppers and Carmine looked at one another and realized there wasn't any tactful way to broach the subject. So Peppers just blurted it out. "Clifton's offering us a bonus of ten grand each to ignore you altogether and just torch the fucking club asap."

If the goombahs were braced for an angry reaction, they were disappointed. Bert's reply was mildness itself. "I'm not surprised. He's a sneaky little twat, let's face it. And it's a fairly generous offer. Ya gonna take it?"

Fumbling a bit, Carmine said, "Hey, we ain't gonna do nothin' wit'out we talk to you first."

"I appreciate that. And now you've talked ta me. An' I think y'oughtta take the offer."

"Ya do?" said Peppers. The approval should have made him happy but instead it made him nervous. It shouldn't have come this easily.

"Sure, why not take the money? As for Lou, what's he care? Long as things work out, he doesn't even have to know. So when ya plannin' on doin' it?"

The question caught the two thugs unprepared. They hadn't expected things to move so quickly. They thought there'd be some hemming and hawing, more complications, more delays. Suddenly the game was speeding up on them. Peppers cleared his throat and said, "Um, late tonight I guess."

"Tonight," echoed Bert. He slowly bent down to pick up his dog and began meditatively stroking its head. "Tonight. Okay, the sooner the better. But can I make one small recommendation based on local knowledge that you'd have no way of otherwise possessin'? I don't think it should be tonight."

"How come?" said Carmine.

"It's Friday."

"What of it?" Peppers asked.

"Friday night there's extra cops around the docks." This was not true, but it was the first thing the old man thought to say. Feeling that he could do better, he went on, "Plus the fishing boats come in on Friday night with those big whaddyacallits, the big arc lights they use. Friday night's a bad idea."

"Tomorrow night at the latest then," said Peppers.

"Yeah, tomorrow night would definitely be better," Bert agreed. He petted the chihuahua. He gazed appreciatively off to the west, where the vanished sun had left behind a few pink clouds stretched out against a swath of yellow sky. Then he said casually, "Ya given much thought to your alibis?"

"Alibis?" said Carmine. "Our alibi is that no one's gonna see us and by the time the fire trucks get there we're gonna be halfway up the Keys."

The old man squinted toward the horizon. "Excuse me, but that does not constitute an alibi. That's just wishful thinking that everything comes off perfect. Look, I don't wanna see you guys get in any trouble. So let's think a couple things through, okay? Gas. Ya got the gas yet?"

"Nah, we'll pick it up tomorrow," Peppers said.

"In what?"

"Whaddya mean, in what? We'll buy a gas can when we buy the gas."

Bert peered at the water. There were coppery glints on the tops of the wavelets, long troughs of glassy black between them. "Nah," he said, "this I don't like."

Carmine had propped a beefy leg on a bollard and was leaning his thick torso across it. "What? What don't you like?"

"You guys buyin' a gas can. I mean, think about it. Two guys who obviously do not live here and therefore have no need of, say, a generator or a lawn mower, buy a brand new gas can in full view of several employees plus the security camera that every retail place in town has one, then a joint mysteriously burns down, and the strangers don't even have an alibi for where they were except now they're haulin' ass in the opposite direction from the scene of the crime. That's what I don't like."

This was hard to disagree with. Peppers pinched his lips together tightly. Carmine rubbed the stubble on his chin.

Bert said, "So I'll bring the gas can."

"You?" said Carmine.

"I always keep a spare inna garage. We do get hurricanes here, ya know. Outages. Shortages. Nothin' suspicious about an old local wit' a gas can."

Peppers ran a hand across his concave face. With rather grudging gratitude, he said, "Okay Bert, good thinkin', thanks. We'll pick it up from you tomorrow."

"No you won't. Don't you guys listen? I said I'd bring it."

"Bring it?" Carmine said. "Bring it where?"

"To the club. Where else? I'll stash it. You guys shouldn't be seen with it. You won't touch it till it's time to do the deed. Much safer that way."

Peppers said, "Listen, Bert, that's awful nice but you don't have to—"

"Yeah, I do have to," the old man interrupted. "Look, I still got an obligation here, a promise to Lou to help you guys. An' there's still some details that have to get worked out. But we'll figure on late tomorrow night, once the joint is closed. No more stalling and no more complications. Agreed?"

39

Bert lingered a while at the Celebration after Peppers and Carmine had peeled off and headed back to their hotel. Then he strolled through downtown and up to Titters. It was around nine o'clock when he arrived to swap updates and plan strategy with his unlikely allies. He was still there, his dog asleep on a table, at two in the morning.

By that time, Marsha had filled up half a yellow pad with notes and diagrams. She and Pat and Lenny had gone over every square inch of the cluttered old club—the stage, the bar, the disused engine room, the entrances and exits. They'd checked out every nook and cranny and lookout spot and hiding place; they'd considered escape routes and where the gas can could most conveniently be stashed. Pat had walked and gestured through various scenarios like a director blocking out a theater piece. Lenny had stood in as Ricky up on stage; Marsha counted the number of steps it would take for his would-be assassin to close the distance between them; Bert guesstimated how many chairs and tables would be turned over in the process. They considered how to assure a good turnout and how to include in the festivities a certain person they didn't much like.

When they were all too tired to see straight, Bert stood up to end the meeting. "Well," he said, "it ain't the tidiest plan I ever saw. In fact, it's kind of a mess. But it's a start. Course, there's more details to be worked out."

With Bert there were always more details. He roused his snoring dog and left.

Outside, on US 1, he stood at the curb and waited for a taxi to come by. None did at that late hour. But after a couple of minutes a pink Pedi-Cab appeared. He hailed it and climbed in.

The Pedi-Cab's back seat was curved and cozy and lushly padded. The quiet residential streets south of the highway were fragrant with the ripening of next day's flowers and the light from the streetlamps was softened into lavender globes by the mild and humid air. It should have been a very relaxing ride, but Bert could not relax. He was bothered by certain aspects of the so-called plan that just hadn't been resolved up to his standards. Mulling, he absently stroked Nacho between the ears and watched the regular, hypnotic motion of the driver's legs pumping up and down as he pedaled the bike. The legs were clad in a purple leotard and were beautifully muscled like the legs of a ballet dancer.

At some point, seemingly out of nowhere, Bert said to the driver, "'Scuse me, buddy, but how fast can this thing go?"

The driver kept pedaling as he looked back across his shoulder. He had a pleasant boyish face whose most natural expression seemed to be a playful if not flirtatious smile. "Why, you in a hurry?"

"No, just curious."

"Not super-fast. Fast enough."

"Faster than a man can run?"

"Once it gets going, yeah, I think so. Faster than most guys can run, I think." With a shrug, he swiveled forward and continued on.

After a moment, Bert said, "Can it roll okay on a dock?"

"Excuse me?"

"Like, at Garrison Bight, where the houseboats are. Can this thing go down there?"

"Long as there's a ramp, sure."

Bert rubbed Nacho's head. "What would it cost to rent it for a couple hours?"

"Hey, you can hire me for as long as you like. Eighty dollars per."

"Thanks, but here's the thing. No offense, you're very pleasant company and all, but I don't need a driver, just the bike. How 'bout for the bike alone?"

The young man with the great legs glanced dubiously at the ancient fellow in the passenger seat. "You gonna pedal it yourself?"

"Never mind who's gonna pedal it. How much would it be to rent?"

"Well, jeez, I'm not supposed to do that. I mean, I don't own the thing. I just take it out for shifts. I'm not supposed to leave it unattended."

"Okay, I understand. Mind if I ask what your name is?"

"Danny."

"Danny, listen, I would never ask a person to do something that he ain't supposed to do, but how about I pay you five hundred bucks to park the bike in a certain place at midnight tomorrow and then you wander off and have a couple drinks or something? Rest your legs a while. I mean, would there be any harm in that?"

Effortlessly pedaling, flashing the playful grin, Danny said, "Well, no, I guess not. Not if I didn't get caught."

"Deal, then?"

"Five hundred cash?"

"Five hundred cash."

"Okay, deal." He pedaled another block or so. Moonlight flashed between palm fronds, throwing shadows that were improbably crisp.

"Oh, and Danny," Bert resumed, "there's one more little thing. I'm gonna need the leotard."

"Excuse me?"

"The leotard. I need it."

"*This* leotard?"

"Yeah, that leotard. Could you take it off, please?"

"Now wait a second—"

"Don't get me wrong, young fella. I'm not makin' any kind of what is currently fashionable to call unwanted sexual advances. It's just, like, for a gag, okay? Tell ya what, let's make it seven-fifty and throw in the leotard."

40

"**A**ny more staples?" Marsha asked.

It was barely ten o'clock next morning, and she and Lenny were already down on Duval Street, tacking flyers onto utility poles and palm trees and the bulletin boards of cafes and bars. The flyers had been hastily run off in Pat's office in the perfect yellow house. They said:

>KILLER COMEDY SHOW AT TITTERS
>GUEST STAR DIRECT FROM
>NEW YORK CITY
>NO COVER
>TWO DOLLAR COCKTAILS
>ONE DOLLAR DRAFTS
>IF YOU DON'T FEEL LIKE LAUGHING
>JUST COME FOR THE CHEAP BOOZE

Reaching into the bottom of his backpack for the staples, Lenny said, "Boy, this really takes me back."

"What does?" asked his wife, as she loaded another row of tacks into the gun.

"Putting up posters. Doing free shows. Doing almost anything, practically begging just to get people to listen to your stuff."

Marsha shot a staple through the fourth corner of a flyer. It made a satisfying snap as it bit into a pole. "Or in this case, just getting in enough bodies to make sure the room is glutted up."

They moved to the next pole down the street, through a gradually thickening crowd of early drinkers and window shoppers and people too sunburned from the day before to get out on the beach. "Yeah," mused Lenny, "getting people in a room. That's what it generally comes down to. Which is really kind of amazing if you think about it. That people will show up, I mean, to listen to what you have to say. How many people get that privilege in life—having strangers pay attention to their stuff and maybe laugh or maybe even think about it afterwards?"

"Hand me another flyer," Marsha said. She was on a roll and kept on stapling.

Lenny was on a different kind of roll and kept on musing. "Back in New York, when I got in such a lousy mood...Well, okay, things weren't going so well, but you know what I think really happened? I forgot how lucky I was. I started taking things for granted. Like the luck I'd had so far was just a down payment on what the world still owed me. Which is bullshit. The world's already given me more than I probably deserve."

They weaved down another block. Duval got noisier and more thickly laden with smells of sunscreen and stale beer. Some Harleys roared by. The Southernmost Choo-Choo crawled past, carrying another load of tourists from the cruise ships. Marsha, honed in on the task at hand, scanned the sidewalks and the entryways of shops to see where she could hang more flyers.

Lenny, dogging her steps and leaning forward in that avid way he had when he was talking, said, "But you haven't really been hearing what I'm saying, have you?"

"Sure I have. You've finally been admitting that you're really lucky that people pay attention to your work."

"Not exactly, Marsha. I mean, that's not the main thing I've been saying. Or trying to say. Or thinking." He reached up and gently took her wrist, the one that was holding the staple gun. It was the only way he could think of to get her to stop stapling for a moment. "What I'm talking about is feeling lucky in my life. Which means us. Which means you. Which means how we are together. You're my luck, Marsha. I forgot that for a little while."

"Glad you remembered."

"If I ever forget again, snap a towel against my ass or something."

"A wet, heavy towel. That would be my pleasure." She kissed him on the cheek. Then she freed the wrist that held the staple gun. There were more posters to put up.

⛱ ⛱ ⛱

Around noon, Bert the Shirt sashayed past a pair of secretaries and continued straight on through to Ted Clifton's inner office.

"For Christ's sake, Bert," said its occupant when the visitor was already well beyond the threshold, "this is the second time you've just barged in here uninvited."

"Right," the old man agreed, "and the last time I did it you got even by assaulting my dog. But let's put that behind us and be nice today. May I please sit down? I have some news you're gonna wanna hear."

Grudgingly, Ted Clifton put aside some papers and motioned his visitor toward a chair. Bert didn't sit down right away. First he very deliberately placed the chihuahua on the same corner of the businessman's gleaming desk where it had been the visit before. Then he re-tucked the tails of the lucky shirt he'd worn for the occasion, a silk job with a pattern of craps dice all coming up sevens. When he was finally seated, he said, "I'm happy to tell you that Pat is now leaning very strongly toward giving you the lease."

Clifton seemed deeply unimpressed with this bit of information. His upper lip curled into a smirk and he gave a skeptical lift to one of his eyebrows. "*Leaning very strongly,*" he mimicked. "What the hell is that supposed to mean? Nothing. It means nothing. Just more bullshit and more games and more stalling."

Bert ignored that. "She has a small favor she wanted me to ask of you."

"A favor? She has the gall at this point to ask me a favor?"

"She's putting on a special show tonight. Kind of an all-or-nothing thing. Asking the local A-list comics to come in. Bringing down a surprise guest from New York. She'd like you to be there."

The invitation only made Clifton more annoyed. "Well, I don't want to be there. I have zero interest in her goddamn show."

"It's important to her."

"What do I care? And why the hell's it matter if I'm there?"

Bert leaned forward very slowly and put his yellowish hands flat on the businessman's desk. "Ted," he said softly, "I know this is hard for you to fathom, but she happens to believe in what she's doing. She thinks there's some value in it. She's hoping for one more shot at getting you to agree, maybe work with her somehow, help the place succeed."

"That place will never succeed. That place was custom-made to fail. And I'm not interested in failure. Never have been. Never will be."

Bert shrugged. "Okay. Fine. Some people only bet on favorites. I don't see the fun a that, but there it is. Anyway, Pat wanted me to tell you that if you come see the show and it doesn't change your mind, she'll give it up, she'll sign over the lease. Right then and there. She says you should bring the papers."

Clifton folded his arms and thought that over, his right thumb twitching against the trademark on his perfect cotton sweater. He brightened for some fraction of an instant but then narrowed down his pink-rimmed eyes and said, "And why the hell should I believe she'll follow through on that? Because she's *leaning strongly*? What if she changes her mind? What if she's just jerking me around?"

"Then I guess you will have wasted a couple hours listening to comedy. Maybe even had a few laughs."

The man behind the big clean desk seemed very far from laughing.

Bert paused a moment then reached over, petted his dog, and went on very casually. "And if Pat doesn't do like she says she'll do, then we're on to Plan B, which is all set up and ready to go."

Clifton kept a studiously blank expression on his blandly almost-handsome features.

Bert said, "Come on, you know all about Plan B."

"I have no idea what you're referring to."

The dog started licking its ass.

"And get your fucking chihuahua off my desk."

Bert did as he was asked and cradled Nacho in his lap. "Ted, can we talk? You don't like me. I'm fine wit' that. I don't like you either. But business is business, and we got business to do. No hard feelings that you tried to go around me wit' Lou and then you tried to go around me wit' Peppers and Carmine. Bottom line, it didn't work. So I know all about Plan B and I know you know all about Plan B. But here's the part that might surprise you. I happen to agree with it."

Guardedly, tentatively, with so little breath behind the words that it seemed they could be sucked back with the smallest inhalation, Clifton said, "You do?"

"I do. It's time. If Pat goes back on her word and doesn't sign the papers, then yeah, it's time. But can't y'even find the decency to let her take a shot, save face, keep some dignity? Go to her show. It's no-lose, Ted. If by some miracle ya change your mind—"

"I won't," he interrupted.

"All right then, if she signs the papers, that makes life way less messy for everybody. If she doesn't sign, well, you know what's gonna happen next."

"No I don't. Remember that, Bert. I don't know what'll happen next. I never said I did."

"Fine. Stick to that. The boys and me will be heading over there around eleven. We'll save ya a front-row seat."

41

Back in bed after a room-service lunch, Ricky was nuzzling Carla's ear. This didn't feel at all unpleasant, and neither did his warming breath against her neck, but still, she put a discouraging hand against his shoulder and wriggled an inch or two away from the caress and toward her own side of the bed. "Sorry, Ricky. I just don't feel like it right now."

"Oh," he said. "Okay." It had been quite a while since he'd been turned down but it took him almost no time at all to remember how much he didn't like it. He indulged himself in a brief pout then gave Carla a long moment to feel guilty for the rejection. Finally he said, "It's just, you know, with Carmine and the show and the whole live bait scenario, I'm feeling all keyed up."

She lifted a corner of the sheet and spun out of bed. The movement wasn't abrupt, exactly, but there was a certain angular resolve in it. Looking back at him, her voice gradually rising more than she expected it to, she said, "I'm sorry about that. I really am. But Ricky, it's not my job to keep you un-keyed up. Or un-paranoid. Or un-anything. It's your job. And I really think that if you keep trying to pawn it off on someone else, you're gonna push away a lotta people by the time you're done."

He propped another pillow under his head and gave a thoughtful tilt to his chin. But the attempt at a calm expression couldn't quite mask the hurt feelings or the fact that his first reaction to having his feelings hurt was to get angry and strike back. "Wow, where the hell did that come from?"

She didn't answer. She'd found some clothes and was starting to get dressed.

"I mean, did I say or do anything to deserve that? I don't think I did. I'm trying to make love to you, you start unloading on me. I just don't get that, Carla."

She'd pulled her shorts on and was buttoning a blouse. "Oh, were we making love? I thought it was more like you were taking a tranquilizer. Listen, Ricky, we're both on edge. We're dealing with it differently. You need what you need and I need what I need. What I need is some air. Some light. What I don't need right now is looking at the ceiling. I'm going out. Alone. I'll see you later."

⚓ ⚓ ⚓

"Hol' on, wait a sec," said Peppers, shielding his eyes from the late afternoon glare that came skidding across the water. "*That's* gonna be our alibi? That we were there the whole time?"

"Best alibi there is," said Bert.

He was sitting in his aluminum folding chair at his favorite spot on Smathers Beach, a place where a stub of stone jetty made the wavelets fold back on themselves so that their tops rose up in steep little points like the curlicues on Dairy Queen. Nacho, in sunglasses with blue lenses, was watching with rapt interest as sandpipers ran away from little squirts of breaking surf.

Carmine said, "'Scuse me, Bert, due respect, but I don't see where sittin' right there inna place we're gonna torch is really the best alibi."

"Ya don't? Well, lemme ask ya a question. But first, slide over a step, you're standing in my light. Okay, question. If you're gonna torch a place, ya gotta be there at some point, right?"

"Well, yeah, sure," the big man said.

"And once the job is done, ya gotta get the hell out. Am I right?"

"Well, yeah."

"Okay. So how ya gonna be less whaddyacallit, conspicuous? Waltzin' in and out when there's nobody around for cover, just you and maybe some cops and passers-by and a security camera or two? Or when you're just, like, melting into a crowd, plenty of other bodies around?"

The goombahs just blinked at one another.

"And another question," Bert went on, stroking Nacho between the ears in a spot he stroked so often that the hair was starting to wear off. "Suspiciousness. Say at some point ya gotta justify your presence at the premises where the unfortunate incident occurred. Whaddya say? *'Duh, I just happened to be walking past?'* No. That's lame. Whereas if you can say, '*Hey, I was there all night, I came to see the show*,' then it washes."

Peppers did not seem entirely convinced. He kicked the pointy toe of his black shoe through the thin sand that covered the coral rocks. The toe came out badly scuffed and he hoped he hadn't altogether ruined the shoes. "Okay, so we got a logical reason for bein' there. But still, if we're seen comin' out of a flaming boat—"

"This is why the timing is so crucial," Bert cut in. "Why we gotta do it right at closin' time, when everybody's leavin' anyway. We light the candle. It takes, like, ten, fifteen seconds. We join the crowd moving away, walking, running up the dock. Big confusion. Crowd huddles up. I stay there gawking. You guys slip quietly away. Mission accomplished."

"And the gas?" Carmine asked. "What're we gonna do, hide it under our table?"

"I stashed it already," said Bert the Shirt. "Like I said I would. Stashed it in broad daylight, wit' many locals such as myself walkin' up and down the docks, bringin' various and sundry to their boats. Nobody paid attention. Why would they? It's stashed right next to the back exit, handy as can be. So, you guys have any more doubts or worries you'd like me to address?"

42

Titters had never been half so full.

Maybe it was the posters plastered all over town. Maybe it was the favors Pat had cashed in—the promises to muster friends and family, the free plugs on local radio blaring through a giant bullhorn at the beach. Maybe it was the novelty of talent from out of town. Most likely it was the lure of cut-rate drinks.

In any case, the club started filling up around eight o'clock, and by nine, when the show was scheduled to begin, it was jammed and buzzing. The noise level gradually rose from a companionable hum to a sustained and general roar that carried with it both sore throats and excitement. People jostled at the bar where Pat and Lenny were working side by side; beer foam dribbled over the rims of glasses as elbows bumped together. Marsha and Sam, pressed into front-of-the-house service, led customers to tables and staunchly defended a prime spot in the middle of the room that was reserved for a group of VIPs who'd be arriving later.

Around 9:15, the house lights dimmed and Pat got up on stage, finding the spotlight with the loose, sure tread of a veteran performer. She was wearing jeans and a shimmering silver blouse that shot back glints like flashbulbs. She made a sweeping flourish with the mic, bowed to the applause, then said, *"Welcome, everybody! So glad to see you're all desperate for a laugh. Christ knows I am. But before we start, may I ask you all to please kneel for our national anthem...No, wait, that's the*

NFL. This is Key West. So sit, stand, kneel, lie down with a friend of any race, creed, color, or any one of four thousand eight hundred and sixty-two gender identities. What the hell, if it's okay with the Pope, it's fine by me. So have fun, keep smiling, buy more drinks, and I promise you an evening that you won't forget until after you've forgotten almost everything else."

She introduced the night's first comic, a middle-aged woman with a wild head of tangled gray hair and a pair of flame-red harem pants whose legs were wide enough to hide watermelons in. The comedian launched in on a serious note. *"Tonight I want to talk about progress.*

"Back when I was coming up in comedy...well, not that far up, obviously...But back when I was breaking in, there were hardly any female stand-ups. It was, like, ninety-five per cent guys. One day I asked a male colleague, a buddy, why he thought that was. He thought about it a minute, then he said, 'I'll you why it is. It's because women don't think it's funny not to get laid.'

"So I thought, yeah, all these guy comedians, a big part of their routine is not gettin' any. Can't get a date. Girlfriend won't put out. Wife always has a girdle on. And I had a Eureka moment. No, I don't mean I vacuumed. I did the math. Hey, if there's all these guys not getting laid, there's a roughly equal number of women not getting laid. Why the hell can't we make jokes about it? How about a little parity in the not-getting-laid comedy genre?

"And let's face it, ladies, not getting laid can be a fucking riot. Though, actually, you know what's even funnier? Sort of getting laid. Like, you're in bed naked with a guy and you're still not sure if you've been laid or not. The only clue is that the guy rolls over, lights up a cigarette, and asks you how it was...How what was?

Hey, I hear some laughs out there. Kind of high-pitched, nervous ones. It's okay, girls, laugh! We've all been there, right? Don't squirm, guys. We know you tried your best. Don't get discouraged, that's the main thing..."

⛱ ⛱ ⛱

At around ten-thirty, at the Harbor House, Ricky was still rehearsing his opening in front of the dresser mirror. His eyes were a bit glassy, his pupils dilated, and there was a sporadic twitch at the left corner of his mouth.

Carla was sitting on the edge of the bed, pulling on her shoes. Looking up at his taut reflected face, she said, "I thought we got rid of all the pills."

"Good try. But not quite. I tucked away a little stash. Diet pills. Muscle relaxants. Light stuff. No big deal."

"I thought you were done with all that, Ricky."

"Guess you were wrong. Listen, I'm all keyed up. I told you that. I think I got plenty of reason."

"There's always plenty of reason."

He swiveled in his chair to face her. "Spare me the lecture, and enough with the rescuer bit, okay? I got a show to do."

"A show. Wow. *That's* what you're so keyed up about? A show? Not facing Carmine? That's a little weird, Ricky."

He tugged on his twitching cheeks and said, "Is it? Not to me. Old saying: Dying's easy, comedy's hard. Do you have any idea how long the time feels between setting up a joke and waiting to see if the laugh comes? It's a freakin' eternity. Then, if you do get a laugh, what next? You set up the next bit and wait eternity again. It's very scary. So you stress and work your ass off trying to control it. That's what keys me up. What happens afterwards with Carmine? That's a separate deal. That I know I can't control."

"Maybe I can," Carla said.

He gave his head a skeptical tilt. "Maybe. Maybe you can. Maybe you will. Another rescue job. Seems to come naturally to you."

He turned back to the mirror.

43

There is always curiosity about an empty table in a crowded club, always speculation that perhaps the prime spot is being reserved for bona fide celebrities. So heads turned around 11:30 as Sam threaded her way through the packed house, leading a quartet of late arrivals to their place of honor. But if the others in the audience were hoping for a glimpse of the famous, they were disappointed. The new group comprised a very old man in a loud shirt clutching a chihuahua like a loaf of bread, two young guys who might have been bit players in gangster movies that no one ever saw, and a stiff-looking business type who looked vaguely familiar from around town but inspired no fond associations.

A fresh comedian was just being introduced as the foursome settled in. He was tall and skinny, with thick black-framed eyeglasses and ears that stuck out at right angles like the side-view mirrors on a car. He took the microphone, brought it very close to his lips, flung out his free hand in a wide, ebullient gesture...and then he froze. He said nothing. He did nothing. He didn't move. He didn't blink. Ten seconds passed. A couple of people coughed. After ten more seconds, there were some murmurs, some squeaks from shifting chairs. After half a minute, a smell of nervous sweat began to be noticed in the room, the smell of discomfort and dread that people give off when witnessing a wreck or someone dissolving right before their eyes.

After forty-five seconds, the comedian dropped his outstretched arm, smiled, and said, "Thank you. I call that piece Anticipation. *Can kind of drive you crazy, right? Me, I spend a lot of time thinking about all* the things that can drive a person crazy. Not the obvious ones. Nuclear annihilation, Florida sinking underwater. Truth is, nobody goes crazy over stuff like that. Too big. Too impersonal. It's the little stuff that makes you crazy. Grape skins getting caught between your teeth. Then when you try to floss 'em out, the floss breaks and you got this tiny thread hanging on your gums. It's like fifty times smaller than a pubic hair, but it's taken over your world. It's all you can think about. It's ruining your life. So you reach in with your thumb and finger, and now it's already starting to get unhygienic because you remember that just a little while ago you shook hands with a guy who has a cold. But you're committed, so you reach in with the thumb, and it pushes your tongue aside, so now you can't stop thinking about your tongue. How it just kind of hangs there in your mouth. How does it just hang there? That seems weird, right? So you start moving it around, you can't stop. Then that stringy little purple thing underneath starts getting irritated..."*

At the VIP table, only Peppers was laughing. He said to Carmine, "What, you don't think this guy's funny? He's different. He's fuckin' wit' our heads."

"I ain't heard a single joke," the big man said. "What kinda comedian can't tell a joke?"

"Milton Berle," said Bert. "Now he could tell a joke. He'd just look at ya and open his eyes real wide, ya'd wet your pants."

Ted Clifton said nothing. He wasn't listening to the conversation and he hadn't been listening to the comedian either. He'd been looking around the room, doing a rough head-count of the guests. For just a moment it almost seemed a shame to him that Titters was maybe starting to catch on, finally, right before it closed. Who knew? Maybe, given enough time, the place could actually work. But it wasn't his problem and he didn't waste a lot of time or energy on the thought. He had the lease papers in his pocket, along with an expensive pen. He made a mental note to make sure he got the pen back once the papers had been signed.

⚓ ⚓ ⚓

Backstage, Lenny and Marsha were putting the finishing touches on a maze-like obstacle course with lots of booby traps. There were places where microphone booms could suddenly be dropped like traffic barriers, sharp turns where loops of wire could be pulled taut at ankle level, straight-aways where a hell-bent pursuer might run into a rolling costume rack full of get-ups for the drag shows. There was a rusty locker just wide enough for Marsha to squeeze into while she choreographed the mayhem, and an ancient engine housing for Lenny to hide behind when crouching at the ready with his phone in camera mode.

Outside, shortly after midnight, on the dock leading to Titters' back exit, Ricky and Carla stepped around a driverless pink Pedi-Cab and climbed the short ramp to the stage door. Next to it, neatly tucked behind a concrete post, was a red gas can with a vented cap and a cheerful spout like a child's drawing of a tea-kettle.

As arranged, Ricky knocked three times, paused, then knocked louder, twice. Lenny opened the door, pulled the two of them inside, handed Ricky a purple leotard, and showed him where to dump his street clothes when he quick-changed and fled. Then Marsha led them on a tour of the winding, twisting path through the seemingly random clutter. "Your escape route," she explained. "I'd memorize it if I were you. Walk it three, four times. Got it?"

🌴 🌴 🌴

Pat announced last call just before the headliner was scheduled to come on, then, moving counter to the flow of bodies drifting toward the bar, she sidled over to the table where the VIPs were seated. Flashing a gracious, all-inclusive emcee smile, she said, "How's the show? Everybody having fun?"

Carmine grunted.

Peppers said, "Pretty funny." Then he stopped himself, afraid it might be undignified to show so much enthusiasm.

Pat said, "How about you, Ted? You impressed?"

Grudgingly, the businessman said, "Nice show. Nice turnout."

"Nice enough to change your thinking?"

"No. Not even close. But I'm happy to see you go out on a high note."

He pulled some papers from his pocket and smoothed out their creases with the heel of his hand. He managed something approaching a smile as he passed the pen to Pat.

She took it and leaned over the document, very briefly perusing its contents. With a resigned sigh, she pulled back the sleeve of her shimmering silver blouse. She brought her fingers very close to the dotted line.

Then she said, "No. Uh-uh. Sorry, Ted. I've decided not to sign."

"You what?"

"I've decided not to."

"But you said—"

"I said I was leaning toward signing. But come on, Ted, you're a business guy. Look around. Could you walk away just as something is turning the corner? I can't give up now. Forget it."

Clifton said nothing. His face went from its usual veal-like pink to a congested and unwholesome purple. His blotchy neck swelled and throbbed against his collar.

The house lights blinked three times then gradually began to dim. Pat smiled and said, "Well, that's my cue. Gotta go." She turned and walked away. She still had the pen.

Clifton scowled at her back, looked down at his unsigned papers. "That bitch."

"Zat any way ta talk?" said Bert.

"She lured me in here just to jerk me around and make us look like idiots."

"Speak for yourself," the old man said. He petted his dog and looked at Carmine and Peppers. "I don't happen to think we look like idiots. I think we look like guys who were hoping to avoid unpleasantness. It didn't work. Such is life. So let's not get our bowels in an uproar. We got a plan. Everything is right on schedule. Let's just stay calm and get it done."

44

Onstage again, radiant in the spotlight and glowing in the success of the evening, Pat waved the microphone and blew kisses to the cheering audience. *"Thank you all so much for being here. Thank you for laughing. And now it's my great pleasure to introduce a performer who many of you will recognize from his frequent guest appearances on shows like* Wasted Education, Naked Suburb, *and* Back in My High School Bedroom. *A regular at top clubs on both coasts. Soon, God willing, to star in his own network series. Ladies and gentlemen, direct from New York City, let's give it up for...Ricky Reed!"*

At the mention of the name, Carmine grabbed the edges of the VIP table hard enough to make the glassware rattle.

The room crackled with applause and the stamping of feet against the floorboards as the comedian bounded out from behind the makeshift curtain.

Carmine said, "Holy shit, it's really him!"

Innocently, Bert said, "Who?"

"The little pissant clown that stole my girlfriend."

Onstage, Ricky paced and swooped. *"Thank you, thank you. Such a pleasure to find myself in Key West. Actually, it'd be a pleasure to find myself anywhere. Been looking for years. No real clues yet."*

Carmine said, "I'm gonna kill him. I'm gonna fucking kill him." He put his palms flat out in front of him and made a move to rise.

Bert reached out a gnarled but still strong hand and grabbed him by the wrist. "Here? Now? In front of like a hundred witnesses? Slow down, Carmine. Think."

"Remember that test we all took in school? The one that matched you to your dream career? Mine came back terrarium designer. I thought, great, this is what I was born to do? Put different-colored pebbles in an aquarium that doesn't even have water in it, and now and then drop in a turtle?"

Carmine's breath was coming in quick hard pants. His lips pulled back and showed the edges of his teeth. "As soon as the asshole's routine is over then. I got him. He's mine. You're gonna help me, Peps. You promised."

Peppers didn't look happy but he gave a solemn nod.

"So I go to the guidance counselor. He says, 'Don't take it so hard. It's not like it's your only shot in life. Let's look at your top three'. He riffles through some papers. 'Okay, number two. Goatherd.' This was in Newark, New Jersey. Great place to be a goat, right? So I'm looking at the window, wondering if it's high enough to be worth throwing myself out of."

Ted Clifton bent low over the table and said, "Look, I don't know or care about your little personal issues, but you guys have a job to do. That comes first."

"No it don't," said Carmine.

Clifton looked to Bert to make his case. Bert petted his dog and shrugged.

"So the guy riffles some more papers. 'Ah,' he says, 'here's number three. Vice-President.' So I think it over. Hmm. 'Any idea where I can get a good deal on some turtles?'"

His voice thinned out by exasperation, Clifton said, "Look, we have a deal. If Mr. Benedetti hears—"

"Do me a favor and shut up," said Carmine.

The businessman pulled back like a poked clam.

Soothingly, Bert said, "Relax, Ted. These guys got more pressing business. The other, don't worry. I'll take care of it."

"You?"

Onstage, a fast segue. "But, hey, enough about me. Anybody having a birthday today? Ah, there, you in the back. Nice. Happy birthday, schmuck!"

Carmine had started easing back his chair, putting himself in position to spring up. There were six other tables between him and the stage, no straight aisle between them. Then it was maybe three strides from the stage to the curtain behind it. He guessed it would take around ten seconds to close the distance.

"Okay, enough about him. Back to me. I've always been kind of a glass-half-empty guy. I admit it. Got it from my family. Every time we got together, every phone call, it was always about who died, who caught cancer, whose vasectomy went wrong and their testicles swelled up like cantaloupes. If they didn't have any big bad news, they settled for small bad news. 'Remember Aunt Fay? She can't move her knuckles...'"

The routine rolled along. Some bits got laughs, some bits didn't, but over time there came a momentum that broke down the listeners' resistance and barged past their defenses; that peeled away the membranes around the guilty and neurotic secrets that at the start of the set had felt like private burdens but turned out to be the common property of everyone in the room. Ricky knew how to milk that momentum, knew when to strut, when to pause, when to pivot to a next idea so that small truths would be revealed with the sudden sharpness of a slap and tension would let go in a burst of helpless guffaws. His tempo gradually quickened, jokes blending seamlessly with self-revelations that morphed back into punch lines. His volume crept up, his movements on stage became a manic blur, and by the time the routine ended his shirt was splotched with sweat.

The applause swelled up long and loud, spiked with hoots and whistles. Ricky acknowledged it with a deep bow, then another, then a raising of humbly pressed-together palms and a Hindu-style tilting of his head. He slipped the microphone back into its stand, flashed a final smile to all corners of the room, and started running for his life.

45

The crowd was just beginning to disperse when Carmine and Peppers sprang up from their seats and bolted toward the stage, their progress slowed by rising bodies and shifting chairs. Carmine lowered his shoulder like a fullback and bulled his way through, cursing and being cursed at in return. Tables toppled. Glassware smashed. Ice cubes skittered across the floor.

The killers clambered up the pair of steps that led onto the stage. Spotlight beams threw sinister and distorted shadows that tracked them as they sprinted across the bare platform, their footsteps heavy and hollow on the boards, heading for the slender gap in the black curtain that Ricky had passed through only moments before.

Just before they reached it, Lenny, crouched under a desk, shoved a costume rack across their path.

The goombahs went down hard in a heap of sequins, gold lame, and feather boas. Scrambling to their feet and waving away bits of fluff, they tried to get their bearings in nearly total darkness. Not more than fifteen feet away, a dim red Exit sign glowed feebly. As they made their way toward it, Marsha, cozy in her locker, twitched a cable that brought mic stands raining down against their shoulders and set broken barstools rolling toward their shins. By the time they reached the exit they were bruised and winded and a precious minute had been lost.

But Carmine was not discouraged. He had no doubt that he would find Ricky Reed just outside the door, probably smoking a cigarette or maybe a joint, and then the only problem would be deciding whether to pummel him to death, drown him, or just knock him unconscious and cart him away to be finished off at leisure.

Muscles clenched, belly on fire at the prospect of revenge, the big man flung the door open. It groaned on its hinges but on the other side of it there was no sign of Ricky. There was just an empty dock and a swath of the flat and viscous water of Garrison Bight twinkling copper in the moonlight.

Carmine stood there, fists on hips, chest heaving. Peppers looked around, then pointed. Maybe fifty yards away, bouncing and clunking over the planks of the dock, a pink Pedi-Cab was in retreat.

The two thugs went racing after it.

⛱ ⛱ ⛱

Seething at the VIP table in the quickly emptying club, Ted Clifton said, "Those asshole losers. Those completely unprofessional asshole losers."

"Crime a passion," Bert said with a man-of-the-world shrug. "Always gonna take priority. Human nature."

The businessman said nothing, just grumpily slapped at his pockets as if he'd suddenly noticed that something was missing. "And that dyke bitch walked off with my pen."

"Stop wit' the name-calling, Ted, it stinks a sore losing. Very unbecoming. But come on, ya got no reason to be upset. Your job's gonna get done. I tol' ya that. I'm gonna handle it." He paused a beat, then added, "All you gotta do is hold my dog."

The fastidious Clifton looked with loathing at the small creature smugly curled in its master's lap. He'd seen the dog with its tongue in its ass. He'd seen it nibbling on its tiny penis. He said, "I don't want to hold the fucking dog."

"Look, Ted, I only got two hands, okay? We got the perfect opportunity here. Plenty a people still hangin' 'round in front. Pat's schmoozing everybody as they leave. Nobody's in back. We slip back there, ten seconds and we're done, we walk around the side and join the crowd."

"Why don't I just stay here then?"

"Why? Because I don't trust you with my dog is why. Nacho doesn't leave my sight. Look, Ted, you wanna forget the whole thing, no skin off my ass. But this is the opportunity. Here and now."

The goombahs failed to gain much ground against the fleeing Pedi-Cab until the dock took a sharp left turn and became a steeply inclined ramp.

At that point the driver in the purple leotard began to strain against the pedals, thighs laboring as his butt lifted from the seat, arms clenching for leverage, and the men on foot started closing distance with every stride. Twenty more flat-out paces brought them close enough to see that there was only a single passenger on the wide back settee. Ten more steps revealed that the passenger was a woman; another five brought Carmine close enough that he could clearly see her black hair shining in the moonlight.

A burst of adrenaline gave his legs one final push, and with a headlong dive like something out of Ben-Hur he grabbed the chassis of the Pedi-Cab and held on for dear life. His weight and the clicking drag of his pointy shoes against the dock boards slowed the vehicle to a crawl and in another few seconds it stopped dead.

The driver silently slid down from his seat and moved a little distance off. No one stopped him. He wasn't part of the scenario; he didn't count. He was just some local in a purple leotard.

Struggling to his feet, straining for breath, Carmine looked up and said, "Hello, Carla." He meant it to sound menacing, but the sight of her had put a lump in his throat. He tried to choke it back but it was like swallowing a shard of bone. "Didn't know you were in town."

"Didn't expect to see you here either."

Icily, afraid his voice might break if he let any warmth creep into it, the big man said, "Where is he?"

"Who?"

"Come on, Carla, don't be cute."

"Look, it doesn't matter where he is."

"Matters to me."

"Well, it shouldn't. Not anymore. I'm leaving him, Carmine."

The words hung in the damp air a moment, seeming to shatter into tiny grains that gleamed pale orange in the mix of moon and streetlight.

Then a voice came from a little higher up the ramp. "You *what?*"

Ricky had turned to face the little group. His eyes were soupy and too bright and his body looked suddenly shriveled where his legs and torso didn't quite fill out the leotard.

Peppers started easing forward to chase down the comedian, then realized that a chase would probably not be necessary. The man who'd stolen Carmine's girlfriend didn't seem to be going anywhere. In fact, transfixed with astonishment and affront at being dumped, he was drifting with a dazed gait down the ramp.

"Sorry," Carla said, when he was half a dozen steps away. "It's a shitty way to tell you. Not the way I would've picked. But it's over, Ricky. I can't be with you. You make me laugh but you're way too selfish. Like, by a lot. Maybe you don't mean to be, maybe you don't even notice. But I can't fix it and I'm not gonna live with it. I wish you luck."

Then, to Carmine, she said, "Don't hurt him. Please. Okay? There isn't any need."

Peppers sidled closer to the man in the leotard, just in case.

Carmine looked down at the dock boards and the black water with its oily sheen. He licked his lips. He suddenly felt extremely shy. Without looking up, he said, "You coming back to me, Carla?"

"I think you know I'm not. We had some good times, Carmine. I'm sorry if I hurt your feelings. Let's just leave it at that, okay?"

There was a silence broken only by the squawking of a nearby gull and the honking of scooter horns downtown. Carmine stared at Carla then dropped his eyes again. He balled his fists and let them relax before clenching them once more. His weight shifted from foot to foot but his body couldn't seem to decide which way to move.

Then Ricky started riffing in a manic, improvised staccato. *"So these two schmucks meet on a dock in the middle of the night. One's dressed like a ballerina, the other looks like a Sopranos outtake. One says, 'Christ, you would not believe what just happened to me. I just got dumped by a woman in, like, a Roman chariot, except it was pink.' And the other guy says, 'Holy shit, wait. A pink chariot? Dumped? On a dock? Was she a brunette? Christ, you too? I mean, what are the fuckin' odds?'"*

Peppers came out with a short quick laugh. He knew he probably shouldn't laugh just then, but he couldn't help it. Carmine glared at him in silence for a couple heartbeats. Then, surprising himself, he laughed too. His laugh started as a grudging grunt, more bitter than amused, but it gradually ripened into a chortle, then a rippling bellow that pulsed out of him in waves and carried off his useless rage and suddenly obsolete jealousy to vaporize in the warm night air. Hearing him laugh, feeling the tension ease out of its clench, Carla started laughing too. For a few seconds the three of them all laughed together, then Carmine stopped abruptly and the others followed his lead.

He said to Carla, "Would you please do that again?"

"Do what?"

"Laugh. So I can listen."

"Just like that? It won't sound natural."

"Do it anyway. Please."

She tried her best. She came out with a sound that was richer than a giggle, more restrained than a guffaw, and whose high notes had the crystal brightness of a bell that has almost finished ringing. The big man closed his eyes to hear. It was a great laugh, a wonderful laugh, but he realized now that it wasn't the only laugh in the world. It was a laugh he used to love to hear from somebody he used to know. He wanted to remember it and he was pretty sure it wouldn't haunt him anymore.

46

A few knots of people were still lingering near Titters' front door, chuckling over favorite moments from the show or just saying long goodnights. But mostly the place had emptied out. Mostly what was left was the smell of beer and the sight of stirred-up dust slowly spinning in the spotlights. Still sitting at the VIP table in the nearly vacant room, Bert said, "So come on, Ted, shit or get off the pot. We doin' this or not?"

Clifton said, "All I do is hold the dog. Correct?"

"Right. And b'lieve me, dog's not gonna like it any more'n you do."

Taking one more furtive glance around the doomed club, the businessman said, "Okay, let's go."

They rose. Bert handed over the chihuahua, which immediately took a nip at Clifton's finger and began clawing at the weave of his expensive sweater. Skirting the stage, the two men slipped behind the bar then through the low doorway to the engine room where it was pitch dark save for the red smudge of the Exit sign. Feeling their way through the shambles left behind by Ricky's fleeing and the goombahs' pursuit, they inched toward it.

When they'd nearly reached the back door, Bert dug into a trouser pocket and came out with a lighter. "Here," he said. "Hold this."

In the dim light of the Exit sign, the businessman squinted with horror at the object. "No way. You said I only have to hold the dog."

"Will you please stop being such a wuss? I'll take it back once I grab the gas. Won't be able to reach into my pocket then."

With a slightly trembling hand, Clifton took the lighter.

Bert eased open the back door, checked to make sure the dock was uninhabited, then reached behind the post that hid the gas can. He swung the container over the threshold of the club, and as he did so, he winced, doubled over, pressed a fist hard against his side, and let out an imperfectly stifled shriek of pain. "Christ, my back! Fuckin' sacro-iliac! Fuckin' spasm. Shit. I can't even stand up straight. You better grab the can, Ted."

The businessman just stood there frozen, the dog pulling loops out of his sweater.

"Grab the can! Can't just leave it sittin' there. Come on, grab it! Gimme the dog."

Panicked, utterly confused, Clifton threw Nacho at its owner. "I'm getting out of here," he said.

"Fine, great, terrific," said Bert, his face tipped upward at a grotesque angle because of his painful hunch. "You leave, I limp away, someone finds the can, everybody knows what's up and you can kiss your chance to torch the place goodbye. Pat wins. You lose. Zat what you want here, Ted? You wanna lose?"

Clifton bit his lip.

"I didn't think so," Bert went on. "So come on, grab the fucking can, light up, and you're outta here a winner. Come on, Ted. Do it."

The man's pink-lidded eyes flicked back and forth between Bert, the gas can, and the doorway. Finally, his greed and spite overcame his cowardly prudence, and he grabbed the can while backing toward the exit, making sure he'd get out of the inferno while leaving the bent old man with the balky spine and helpless dog trapped on the wrong side of the blaze. With unsteady fingers he opened the vent, unscrewed the cap, and poured out a stream of liquid that quickly pooled on Titters' uneven wooden floor. Still backing, he flicked open the lighter and tossed it into the puddle.

The fire did not start all at once. It seemed to inhale for an instant before igniting with a baritone pop. Then it burst into a beautiful green flame that threw a perfect light for the guilty photos that Lenny captured as he sprang out from underneath the desk.

An instant later, Marsha emerged from the locker armed with an extinguisher spewing orange foam.

Within seconds there was nothing left of the attempted arson but a faint alcohol smell and some gobs of fire retardant that bubbled then subsided over the tops of the businessman's ruined shoes.

The shoes gave off a squishing sound as Clifton made a futile grab for Lenny's phone, slipped on the foamy floorboards, and skidded to his knees.

"Very undignified," said Bert, who seemed to have made a miraculous recovery from his backache and was standing perfectly straight and tall above the crumpled figure. "With the lease papers in your pocket, no less. This does not look good at all. The cops, even Key West cops, they're not gonna like the looks a this."

Still kneeling, slipping again as he strained to rise, Clifton hissed, "You set me up, you dago bastard."

Bert shook his head sadly. "Again with the name-calling. Where's it get ya, Ted? You were gonna burn me and the dog to a crisp, but ya don't hear me callin' you bad names. I prefer the high road."

Clifton finally managed to regain his feet. His pants were torn. His sweater had largely unspooled. He said, "Fuck the high road. How much you want for the pictures?"

"Us?" He looked around at Lenny and Marsha before he answered. "We don't want nothin'. But I think ya need to talk to Pat about what it's gonna cost ya. Ya been callin' her a lotta bad names, too. But she's a nice person. Maybe she'll be big about it."

EPILOGUE

"Amazing," said Pat, as the exhausted but happy little group clustered around the bar at the otherwise empty club. "It actually worked."

"Of course it worked," said Sam. "Most basic strategy there is. Get somebody out of position. Divide and conquer."

"And hope no one burns the place down in the meantime," Lenny added.

"Was never any chance a that," said Bert, rubbing his dog's head on the spot where the hair was wearing thin. "Not with that stuff. Wood alcohol with a pinch a roach powder thrown in. Bought it off the guy who runs the cats through hoops at Sunset. Got the idea when I was down there with the tough guys. Gives ya that sexy green flame but hardly any heat. Maybe ya could toast a marshmallow over it."

"Except," said Marsha, "Clifton thought he was pouring hi-test."

"Oh yeah," the old man agreed. "Intention-wise, it was arson, attempted murder, roasting a chihuahua, the whole nine yards. Excellent blackmail material."

"Blackmail?" said Pat. "I never even mentioned the word. Didn't have to. Just told him it would be a nice gesture if he'd re-route the Choo-Choo so that it made a stop at the front door of the club. And have his drivers include some nice promotional patter in their script. And give us free ad space on his cutesy bullshit locomotives. He was quite agreeable to everything."

"A real sport," said Bert, "once ya got 'im by the short hairs."

⚓ ⚓ ⚓

"Well, it almost worked," said Ricky, looking back past the twisted shoulder strap of the purple leotard as he drove the borrowed Pedi-Cab through the quiet streets toward Harbor House.

"Our getaway?" said Carla. "Yeah, it might've worked great if that damn ramp wasn't so steep."

"I wasn't talking about our getaway. I was talking about our love affair. It came pretty close to working."

"For a while," said Carla. She was luxuriating on the broad back seat, her arms spread wide to embrace the endless and uncluttered space of the night. "Pretty short while, really. But hey, who wants a love affair that comes close to working? That almost works. That kind of works. Settling for that, that's what gets people trapped, I think."

Trying his best not to sound bitter, he said, "Well, I guess you're not trapped now."

"And neither are you, Ricky. Y'ever consider the possibility that maybe you're just better off without a girlfriend? Without a serious girlfriend, at least?"

"I don't know," he said. "I've only had fifteen, twenty minutes to get used to the idea."

"Might be worth thinking about. I mean, let's be honest. What's the most important thing to you? Being with someone? I don't think so. It's getting laughs. You're very good at it. It lights you up. It's what you have to give to people. Probably the best of what you have to give. No shame in that. Why not just go with it?"

⚓ ⚓ ⚓

Peppers and Carmine drove through what was left of the night and into the next morning, hardly speaking until they hit the Georgia line. Then Carmine said, "Fucking Florida. Florida didn't show me nothin'."

Peppers didn't see the point of arguing, so he just looked out the window at some spindly pine trees sticking up through spirals of mist. A few miles later, he said, "Fat Lou's gonna be pissed off at us."

"If he is, he is. But he shouldn't be. I mean, we saved him from ending up in business with a real douchebag."

They passed a couple more exits before Peppers spoke again.

"Carmine, I'm glad ya didn't whack the funny man. Just wanted ya to know I'm glad."

The big fellow shrugged and tried to figure why his insides suddenly felt pleasantly warm. Maybe it was just relief about a nasty piece of business left undone. Or maybe it was a kind of secret pride at having found within himself a bit of mercy and, along with it, maybe even a sense of humor. "Yeah," he grunted. "Killing a clown in a ballet outfit. What woulda been the point? Not much glory in it, right?"

⛰ ⛰ ⛰

By noon of that January Sunday, Lenny and Marsha and Ricky and Pat were on a flight up to New York. By nine am on Monday the cast and crew and writers of *Dog Groomer to the Stars* had gathered on a sound stage in Long Island City to begin the shooting of their pilot. Five weeks later, a focus group in Muncie, Indiana pronounced the new show funny and fresh, and the network slated eight episodes for spring.

While not an outright smash, *Groomer* was successful enough that when, later in the year, its star, Ricky Reed, finally went into rehab, the entertainment media jumped on the story and gave the show a big boost leading into its second season.

During the hiatus, Lenny and Marsha, now relatively flush with cash, finally had time to get out and look for the bigger apartment they'd been promising themselves for years. They considered places on West End Avenue and even the previously unthinkable Riverside Drive. Giddily, they realized that fabled precincts—close to Lincoln Center, across from Central Park—were suddenly within their reach, or almost.

And yet they couldn't seem to find a place they really liked. A kitchen layout was flawed, a lobby was pretentious, a foyer wasted too much space. Finally, after yet another long day of shlepping around with a realtor, they sat down over coffee and Marsha said, "You know what, Lenny? All these places we've ruled out, I don't really think it comes down to what kind of knobs are on the bathroom sinks or whether the ceilings have molding. I'm wondering if maybe we can't decide because, deep down, we just don't want to live here anymore."

By reflex rather than conviction, Lenny leaned forward and said, "But we're New Yorkers. New York is where we live."

"Right. And a year or so ago, when you were feeling so miserable and we were fighting all the time, where were we living then?"

"In a small apartment. With a crappy rug."

"Fine. Blame the rug. And when you couldn't stand it anymore, and when we even thought maybe the marriage was falling apart, where did you go?"

"Someplace where I had a friend."

"You have friends lots of places, Lenny. Why'd you pick Key West?"

He sipped some coffee. "Well, for one thing, it was winter. But okay, maybe it was because, up here, everything just seemed so goddamn serious, like the-sky-is-falling serious, and you're supposed to feel guilty, like you're a bad and trivial person if you don't buy into that. Which I didn't. And still don't. So I thought Key West might sort of be the antidote. You know, goofy, light."

"Except," Marsha put in, "for things like Mafia vendettas and occasional acts of arson."

"True, it got a little more serious than I expected. But in a different way. Not big-picture-Armageddon-doom-and-gloom. More like just dealing with what's in front of you, doing the right thing in that moment. Helping your friends. So yeah, I got a little bit more serious."

"And I got a lot less solemn," she admitted. "Out from under the shit-pile of the evening news. Key West sort of brought things back to actual size."

She picked up her coffee cup and half-hid her face behind it before adding, "Ever think of moving there, Lenny?"

It was a question that had been silently simmering for years, but even so it seemed abrupt when spoken out loud and it called forth a nervous laugh. "Hell yeah. All the time. Great fantasy. Great safety valve. *Someday we'll just retire to a little yellow house down in the Keys...*"

"Like, when?"

"Like, I don't know. Later. When we're a little older. Working less hard. Ready to back off a little. Ready to slow down a little."

"Ready to be happy?" Marsha asked.

"Yeah, maybe. Maybe then. Maybe when we're more ready to kick back and be happy."

She raised her coffee to her lips and took a sip. "That place on Amsterdam," she said. "Location's great but the light just wouldn't suit us."

#####

ABOUT THE AUTHOR

Laurence Shames has been a New York City taxi driver, lounge singer, furniture mover, lifeguard, dishwasher, gym teacher, and shoe salesman. Having failed to distinguish himself in any of those professions, he turned to writing full-time in 1976 and has not done an honest day's work since.

His basic laziness notwithstanding, Shames has published more than twenty books and hundreds of magazine articles and essays. Best known for his critically acclaimed series of Key West novels, he has also authored non-fiction and enjoyed considerable though largely secret success as a collaborator and ghostwriter. Shames has penned four New York Times bestsellers. These have appeared on four different lists, under four different names, none of them his own. This might be a record.

Born in Newark, New Jersey in 1951, to chain-smoking parents of modest means but flamboyant emotions, Shames graduated summa cum laude from NYU in 1972 and was inducted into Phi Beta Kappa. Shortly after finishing college, he began annoying editors by sending them short stories they hated. He also wrote longer things he thought of as novels. He couldn't sell them.

By 1979 he'd somehow passed himself off as a journalist and was publishing in top-shelf magazines like Playboy, Outside, Saturday Review, and Vanity Fair. In 1982, Shames was named Ethics columnist of Esquire, and also made a contributing editor to that magazine.

By 1986 he'd made the transition to non-fiction books. His 1991 bestseller, BOSS OF BOSSES, written for two FBI agents, got him thinking about the Mafia. It also bought him a ticket out of New York and a sweet little house in Key West, where he finally got back to Plan A: writing fiction.

With FLORIDA STRAITS, Shames introduced the much-loved character of Bert the Shirt and launched his perennially popular series of KEY WEST CAPERS, of which ONE BIG JOKE is lucky number thirteen.

To learn more, please visit www.LaurenceShames.com

Works by Laurence Shames

Key West Novels—

One Strange Date

Key West Luck

Tropical Swap

Shot on Location

The Naked Detective

Welcome to Paradise

Mangrove Squeeze

Virgin Heat

Tropical Depression

Sunburn

Scavenger Reef

Florida Straits

Key West Short Fiction—

Chickens

New York and California Novels—

Money Talks

The Angels' Share

Nonfiction—

The Hunger for More

The Big Time

Made in the USA
Columbia, SC
17 May 2021